ROLLO AND LIONEL REVEL IN THE SPRING AIR AND SUNSHINE (page 7)

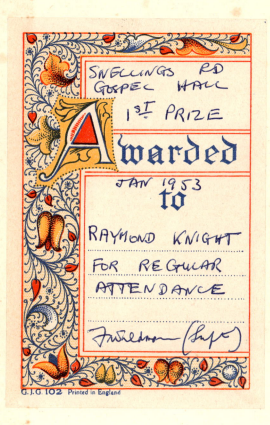

SNELLINGS RD
GOSPEL HALL

1ST PRIZE

Awarded

JAN 1953

to

RAYMOND KNIGHT

FOR REGULAR

ATTENDANCE

J.Wildman (Supt)

G.J.G. 102 Printed in England

TWO TRAMPS

AMY LE FEUVRE

LONDON
PICKERING & INGLIS LTD.

Pickering & Inglis Ltd.

29 Ludgate Hill, London, E.C.4
229 Bothwell Street, Glasgow, C.2
59 Cross Street, Manchester, 2
105 Bold Street, Liverpool, 1
95 St. Mary Street, Cardiff
203 Corporation Street, Birmingham
56 Grainger Street, Newcastle upon Tyne
29 George IV Bridge, Edinburgh, 1
Fleming H. Revell Company, 158 Fifth Avenue, New York, 10
Home Evangel, 418 Church Street, Toronto, 2
Libreria Editorial Cristiana S.R.L., Calle Caa-Guaza 896, Lanus, Argentina

Made and Printed in Great Britain

CONTENTS

CHAPTER I

Uncle and Nephew

H E knew he was being inspected, and with hands in his pockets and legs well apart, he squared his small shoulders and pursed up his lips for a whistle. It was a way of his when—as he expressed it—"I feel a bit shaky!"

Two people had their eyes upon him—his governess and his uncle. He knew Miss Percy well enough to be sure that her criticism of him would be just and fair; but this tall brown-bearded man was almost a stranger, and his eyes were keen and far-seeing.

"Well, what is the matter with him, Miss Percy? He is white and thin, but all Indian children seem that."

"The doctor says his brain is too active, and he must be kept away from books for a time."

"And what do you propose?"

"The doctor suggested sending him into the country for a month or two. He says an open-air life is what he needs."

"Doctors are fond of open air. I have been ordered into the country myself for a couple of months."

" You have not been well ? "

" The usual complaint nowadays—influenza ; but I've had a long case on, which has taken a good bit out of me."

Rollo looked at his uncle with more interest now, though he was being dismissed. He pocketed a five-shilling piece with a radiant smile ; but as he left the room he remarked aloud as if to himself—

"Should think we could go to the country together."

As the door closed on him Lionel Derrick looked at Miss Percy and laughed.

" If he wasn't so small I would take him ; children of that age want a woman to look after them."

" Not for a short time," said Miss Percy, smiling ; "and Rollo is a child of infinite resources."

" What else is he ? "

" Very good company."

" I believe you want me to take him."

" It would be a relief to my mind if you could. I cannot give up my other pupils to go with him myself, and I know of no one to whom I could send him."

" Pack up his things, then, in a small hand-bag, and send him round to my chambers to-morrow morning by eleven o'clock sharp. If I find him a trouble, I can but put him into the train and send him back to you."

This summary conclusion rather startled Miss Percy.

" Where are you going ? " she asked.

" Haven't an idea ; but as far from London as I can. I'm thinking of tramping the country, and sleeping in the open ; that is, if sleep will come back to me, for it has forsaken me at present."

" Rollo's lungs are strong enough, but he has had no

experience of roughing it. Perhaps he does want a woman's care."

"Now I have frightened you, have I not? I promise to look after him, and if the life doesn't suit him I will send him back. Well, I must be going. Good afternoon. Mind that he is punctual."

He swung out of the house in a driving shower of sleet and rain, and Miss Percy looked after him doubtfully.

"I hope I shall be right in letting the boy go. It rather takes my breath away! I know his mother thinks a good deal of Mr. Derrick. It was only in her last letter that she told me she wished he would take more notice of Rollo. And I have always heard that he is a very good young man. His influence will be for good. I suppose he was only in fun when he spoke of tramping the country. After all, it is only for a short time!"

She went in search of her small pupil, and found him alone by the schoolroom window, flattening his nose against the panes, as he watched the retreating figure of his uncle.

"Come here, Rollo dear, I want to speak to you."

The boy turned round. He was defiant no longer. A round, short-cropped head of brown hair, a resolute little mouth, and two of the most lovely eyes that ever a boy possessed were his. "Girl's eyes" his little schoolfellows called them, and certainly such deep blue ones, with their long curled black lashes, would be far more prized by the gentler sex.

Unfathomable eyes they were : eyes that noted everything, and looked away into the unseen and stayed there, until you wondered when they were coming back.

They were looking very frank and fearless now; and Miss Percy smiled into the little questioning face.

" Your uncle is going to take you with him, Rollo."

Rollo nodded wisely. " I thought he might. It would be stupid if I was to go by myself, and he by himself. When are we going ? "

" It seems dreadfully sudden, but he wants you to go to-morrow."

The boy capered in delight. " Tell you what, Miss Percy ! We'll be two travellers, and go through woods, and shoot tigers, and get lost in the desert ! "

" Never mind the tigers, but listen to me ! You are a little boy and you will have no one to look after you, so I want you to remember a few things. First, you can dress yourself nicely, so be always careful to do it. Show your uncle you do not need a nurse. Then never forget —wherever you are—your weekly letter to your mother. Friday is mail day. If it is only three lines, mind you send it. And lastly, never forget your prayers, and be a good boy."

" I'll remember," nodded Rollo ; " is that all ? "

" And read no books while you are away. Those are the doctor's orders."

" Shall we have wet days in the country ? It's the rain makes me want to read. If I'm right inside a book, I forget it's raining."

" We will hope you will have fine weather, then. Now I must go and see to your clothes."

Miss Percy kept a very small school for Indian children. She lived with her mother in one of the quiet streets in Kensington, and had had Rollo in her charge since he was three years old. His father and mother were still out in India, and were almost strangers to him. Lionel Derrick, his mother's brother, was the only relative he had in England. He was a barrister, and beyond an occasional visit to his small nephew had taken but little notice of him. Rollo almost felt as if he were going off with some brigand in disguise, he looked so tall, so stern, so unknowable.

Dilating on his future to the five other small boys who shared Miss Percy's care, he said after the schoolroom tea was over that evening, "And when you fellows are over your sums, and they won't come right, I shall be a pirate king eating rabbits in a gypsy camp, and fighting the robbers on a black horse!"

This seemed such a delicious medley to his audience that they gasped. "And what will you do with your uncle?"

"Tell you what! He isn't my uncle. He is a pretender, and he'll take me to a castle in a forest, where he'll keep me till he gets a ransom. I shall escape and be like Robin Hood. I shall shoot deer with a bow and arrow, and nobody will ever catch me."

With such wild flights of fancies as these, there was not much sleep for Rollo that night. Twice he frightened the other boy who shared his room by jumping out of bed and screaming, "Where's my sword? He's after me! Fly for your life!" And at early dawn he was lying awake, picturing his holiday with all a child's brightness and vividness of colouring.

Miss Percy parted from him with a sigh. He was her baby, her pride; and she blamed herself for the edict

that had gone forth from the doctor's lips. Had she
not pressed the little fellow on, from alphabet to primer,
and primer to ancient history, and taken a keen delight
in feeding the active brain? Now she was to lose him,
and another would have the benefit of his quaint
company.

She delivered him over to his uncle with many a word
of counsel, and Rollo parted with her, feeling a little like
a young bird being ousted from its nest. He held himself bravely, and when once in the railway carriage with
his uncle commenced to prove the assertion of his
governess, that he was very good company.

He crossed his small legs, and produced a sticky
packet from his jacket pocket.

"Will you have one?" he asked confidentially. "It's
toffee—what the fellows gave me this morning."

This was civilly declined.

"Ah! p'raps you like bullseyes? I finished my last
one the day before yesterday. We always buy sweets
when we go in trains. Miss Percy says they're bad for
teeth, but I've just got my new set, so I'm all right."

Uncle and nephew were soon the best of friends. It
is true Rollo did most of the talking. Lionel Derrick
lay back with a tired brain, listening in lazy wonder to
the boyish chatter. But as time wore on Rollo's head
began to ache, and his eyes became surrounded by dark
circles. He battled bravely with his fatigue; headaches
had been his fate for some months past, and he was boy
enough to be ashamed of them.

His conversation changed its tone. From a rollicking
carelessness, a pensive note was struck, and Lionel
looked across in bewilderment, when the small voice

said, "I suppose we shall be able to find a house to sleep in when we get to the country. There don't seem many outside just now. The real country is where there isn't a house for a hundred miles, isn't it? P'raps the first night we can sleep at the station."

"We shall find good beds where we are going, my boy," was the cheery answer.

"That will be first-rate. I think myself I'd like a bed as far away from trains as you could get one."

"What's up? You're as white as a ghost."

"Oh, nothing. I've—I've just a—well, a kind of a headache!"

Poor little Rollo! In another minute, dignity forgotten, he was snuggled on his uncle's knee, and in a very short time the long lashes had closed over the big blue eyes, and he was fast asleep. Lionel, looking down upon the baby face, and feeling for the first time the unconscious weight of the sleeping boy, began to question his wisdom in saddling himself with such an encumbrance, but when he heard the murmured words, "We're going to be roving robbers, he and I," he laughed his fears away, and thought at all events with such a companion he would be no prey to *ennui*.

Two days after, in the heart of Devonshire, uncle and nephew had arranged their tramp.

A small moor pony had been hired for Rollo, and Lionel, with his knapsack on his back, was walking by his side, determining to revel in the sweet Spring air and sunshine, and saunter along the green lanes and open moors, ignoring time, and stopping only when he felt inclined. "We shall be roving robbers if you will," he said with a laugh to Rollo; "but Nature is so lavish with her gifts that we shall not need to steal from her."

"It's what I call stunning!" was Rollo's quick reply. "We shall see different things every day, and do just what we like. It's a pity you haven't a gun."

"I want to be at peace with all, don't you?"

"Well—um—yes—unless we have to fight, you know. There may be masked robbers when it gets dark, and if they have guns we ought to have some too."

"But what could they take from us?"

"Well—I've a three-blade knife, with a corkscrew; I'm sure they'd bag that if they could."

"Keep it dark then, and when they come, hide it in your boots. Are robbers to be our only fate?"

"Of course, a gun is useful to shoot lots of things with," went on the small boy. "We shall have to get some dinner."

"I suppose we shall. The meat sandwiches in my pocket don't suit your taste?"

"Well, you see, sandwiches are what you can get in London. They're rather—rather dull."

"Not spicy enough? What do you propose?"

"I think most travellers like a deer, a few rabbits or some birds."

"I don't aspire to be a traveller. I'm only a tramp."

"Tramps beg."

"Perhaps I shall."

"But s'posing there's nobody to beg from?"

"Then I shall fall back on the sandwiches."

Not very intellectual conversation perhaps, but good for a tired, overwrought brain.

More than once Lionel bared his head, and opened

his mouth to take in as much as he could of the fresh pure life-giving air.

And Rollo rode on, his blue eyes roving from earth to sky; his little heart satisfied and quieted by the breadth and freedom of his vision. Many a halt was made; for those quick eyes saw many an object they wished to investigate more closely; and Lionel lounged along, ready to loiter at the smallest pretext.

The rush of his town life made him appreciate this delicious slow progress all the more.

B

CHAPTER II

Rollo the Scribe

"TELL you what! We'll write a book."

Of course it was Rollo who spoke. His "Tell you whats" always heralded some novel proposition; and Lionel in his dull moments hailed them with delight.

It was eleven o'clock in the morning—a time when the world's labourers were in the midst of their toil—a time when one can fully appreciate the luxury of idleness.

It was a sunshiny morning in the beginning of June. Lounging against a green bank, with a foreground of sweet-scented gorse and moorland, were our two travellers. The pony was tied up near. Lionel, his hat over his eyes, was lying full length on the short, springy turf, Rollo was sitting, his hands clasped round his knees, his blue eyes gazing at the golden bloom. They had been very silent, listening to a lark soaring up in front of them. There was almost a Sabbath stillness around them; no butterflies or bees fluttered above the bloom; in the distance the bleating of the lambs in the meadows was the only sound that met their ears. And then Rollo broke the silence by his speech.

Lionel rolled over with a grunt.   "Write a book!
Why take us back to such commonplaces, that smatter
of Fleet Street and the Strand?   Do you know why
people write books?"

"Because they want to."

"Because they want to air the opinions that they
can get no friend to listen to."

With knitted brow Rollo thought over this view of
the subject.   "But my book would tell people things
that they would like to know."

"That sounds hopeful.   Give me a chapter of
it."

Rollo was silent for a minute, then he said slowly—

"My first chapter would be 'Golden Gorse.'"

"Well done!   A taking title; why not 'Glorious
Golden Gorse'?"

"I think 'Good Golden Gorse.'"

"Why?"

Then the boy's eyes kindled.   "It's so sweet, so soft,
so sunshiny; and it comes out of dry, dead prickles.
I could tell about it being covered up and shut in by
horrid spikes.   It's two kinds of people on the same
bush; it's a golden princess shut up, so that no one
shall get to it."

Lionel looked astonished; then he lay and gazed at
the gorse in front of them.   "We will learn a lesson
from it," he said dreamily.   "Sweetness thriving amongst
bitters.   A narrowed starved confined life, blossoming
out and turning its surroundings into fragrant beauty.
You've given me a thought, Rollo.   Yes, I think we
must write a book together."

"And," pursued the boy, "there's a lot more, only I

can't tell it.   It makes you wish to smell it, to kiss it, and yet you can't."

"Not without hurt to yourself.   Nothing is worth anything without toil and trouble.   Our book will be a philosophical treatise."

"I wish you would talk easier."

Rollo's rebuke was crushing.   Then, relapsing from the dreamer into a very practical boy, he started to his feet.   "I'm going to see if there are any frogs in that ditch over there.   I love frogs, don't you?"

But Lionel could not turn from golden gorse to frogs so easily.   He lay there in the sunshine, and thought of a blossom he knew, dwelling in difficult surroundings—a blossom that he would willingly have transplanted to his own garden, and enjoyed the fragrance of its life.   Yet the bloom would not leave the prickles, and as yet would not allow the young man to approach it.

From philosophy he passed to day-dreams ; from day-dreams to sleep ; and when Rollo roused him at length the sun was at its full height, and the boy insisted that he was hungry.

"Is it lunch time?   Not yet.   I think we will make our way over the moor to that farmhouse.   Perhaps they can give us some eggs and bacon.   We'll have a try."

So Rollo was mounted on his pony, and away they went, cracking the dead heather underfoot and startling many a rabbit from its lair.   They reached the farmhouse within half an hour, but there seemed no signs of life about it.   Leaving Rollo on his pony, Lionel stepped boldly in, and at length found an old woman at her washtub in an outhouse.   He asked her if she could supply them with any food.

" Be 'ee on they cycles ? " was her sharp inquiry.

" No, I am on foot, and my small nephew on his pony."

" Ah, well, 'tis better style. They cyclists is not the gentry, and they holdeth their heads so cocketty, and sniffeth at the country; for 'tis not good enough to plase 'em. And their pockets be brave an' empty. I remembers back along, a party, an' they cometh in and maketh free with a pasty, and drinketh four glasses o' fresh milk, an' when they cometh to go they coodn't find fippence betwixt 'em ! Es, sir, A'll fetch 'ee a plate o' ham, and the little lad can tie his pony to the gate, for the men be all out to the fields, and I be by me lone self, and I be eighty year old, sir, cometh Michaelmas, and I be brave and hearty, thank the Lord."

She showed them into a parlour, which seemed delightful in its coolness after the midday sun. It was a long, low room, with a round table, black horsehair sofa and chairs, and a quaint old cupboard with glass doors, filled with bits of china. Lionel inspected this latter piece of furniture with some interest. It was a curious medley of ancient and modern ware; from penny china dolls and painted dogs to some really quaint old junket bowls. Then there was a bookcase towards which Rollo gravitated with a keen look in his blue eyes, and when he found an ancient mythology with coarse wood engravings he sat down upon the floor with a happy sigh of content. Lionel left the room soon to look to the pony's wants and give him a feed of corn. When he returned he found a white cloth laid, and ample supplies for two hungry people; but Rollo was standing in a corner, his back against the wall, his hands behind him, and his eyes looking away into space.

" What's up ? " the uncle asked.

Rollo lowered his gaze, but he did not move from his position. " I'm trying to be a man of honour," he said gravely.

" Be a boy first before you ape the man," was the amused remark. " What is the temptation ? "

" I want to read about the pictures, and Miss Percy told me not to."

" Oh, I see ! Well, the temptation has gone, for the opportunity has come for you to feed your body, and not your mind."

And Rollo proved that he could do this with very little difficulty.

During lunch, black clouds rolled up and soon obscured all the sunshine, and before they could start again on their travels, down came a deluge of rain.

Lionel was in no way disconcerted ; he rolled himself round on the horsehair couch and was soon fast asleep. Rollo looked at him in astonishment, then his glance fell lovingly on the old bookcase, and for a minute he wavered. But honour won the day, and, creeping softly out of the room, the boy made his way to the big, stone-flagged kitchen. The old woman was there making bread. The table was freshly scoured, the fire bright and clear, and the copper pans glistened and reflected like mirrors. Rollo looked up to the wooden beams from which home-cured hams were suspended. Everything was new, and consequently charming to him.

He advanced to the table, and leaning with folded arms upon it commenced to unburden his mind.

" What are you making ? May I watch you ? "

"Bless 'ee, little master, 'tis bread, and a proper batch it be this day! Last Toosday me back were turned but just one minute, and if that old sow didn't cut in, and with her ugly snout make short work o' my dough just a rizzin' bravely afore the fire."

Rollo looked thoughtful, then he said, "Were you ever a tramp on the road?"

"Likely no!" was the somewhat indignant reply. "I be come o' respectibble folk, an' could a bin married four times over had I had a mind to!"

"I like being a tramp. You never know what you're coming to. This morning I didn't know you were in the world at all."

This fact seemed to startle the old woman. She gazed at him wonderingly, then shook her head in doubt.

Rollo pursued his own line of thought dreamily. "And I suppose there are lots of people that I never shall know about till I see them in heaven, but I shan't forget you, for you look so very old."

"I baint near so old as our minister, an' he be ten year younger than I!"

This paradox did not puzzle Rollo. He changed the subject.

Stretching out his hand, he took up a paring of dough and began to mould it absently in his fingers.

"Are you all very old here?" he asked. "I s'pose there aren't any boys like me about?"

"Na, an I woodn't give much to have 'em here. They be too clatterous."

Rollo sank his voice to a confidential whisper. "I'm on the lookout for some. I wouldn't say so to my uncle,

for he's a very good chap, but I ache when I'm talking
grown up too long. I think I don't mind the talking;
but I should like to roll him over and pummel him a
bit—just lark round, you know! My legs want a bit of
a scrimmage. Don't tell him I said so. I s'pose you
haven't a dog, have you?"

"Ay, that us have. Shock an' Daisy; an' they be
brave 'uns fur drivin' sheep an' the like. They be out
in the fields with they master."

"I wish we had a dog," said Rollo, a little wistfully.
"They're so awfully jolly to teach tricks. One of our
fellows at school could make Miss Percy's terrier stand
on his head. Have you finished your bread? When
will it be done? I say, could I walk over the house?
My uncle is fast asleep, and I don't know what to do."

The old woman looked at the little questioner, then
shook her head doubtfully.

"Na, the rooms ain't fur boys; 'ee must bide still an'
not worry. Can't 'ee read or write?"

"I should think I could just!"

"Well, noo, I'm thinkin' maybe 'ee could write a
letter to my John, fur I can niver get the lads to give a
minute to 'em. See here, I'll get a bit o' paper, and
'ee'll sit down an' write fur I, like a little gentleman."

Rollo responded with alacrity to this suggestion, and
soon, with his pen poised between his fingers in the
orthodox fashion, he sat awaiting the old lady's dictation.

She fussed about for a few minutes, putting the
kettles on the fire for tea, washing her hands, and
inspecting her dough, which was now before the fire;
but finally she came and stood over the little scribe with
knitted brows.

"My dear John," wrote Rollo; then he asked, "Who is John? Is he a boy?"

"Ay, the best o' me boys, an' lies to hospital wi' a broken leg. 'Twas his hoss threw him, when he were comin' home from market on a Saturday. I fears he were a bit fuddled wi' the drink. Tell 'un I hopes 'un is quite well as it leaves me at present."

This was written. Then there was a long pause.

"I should tell him it's raining," suggested Rollo, looking out of the window for inspiration.

"Ay, an' Mark Pedley's father have bin caught out poachin' an' have bin took off to gaol."

"Oh! do tell me about that," said Rollo, dropping his pen in his excitement. "I would like to see a poacher. They creep through long grass in the woods, and catch rabbits and birds in the night, don't they?"

"The Pedleys be a bad lot," was the reply. "Mark smashed my Johnnie's nose when 'un were at school. I minds it well. Write it in brave an' plain, an' tell 'un that Jane Trevaunce have a-jilted of Mark."

With a little sigh Rollo turned to business; then came another pause, and the old woman shook her head in desperation.

"Ay, dearie me, a letter be hard. Tell 'un to come home quick."

"And shall I say I'm writing the letter and tell him who I am?"

"Ay, 'ee be a clever little lad. Fill up the paper an' I'll make the end to 'un."

Rollo sucked the handle to his pen, thought for a moment, and then wrote steadily on, spelling audibly the words as he went. The old woman added her last words, and then he read it out in triumph to her :—

"MY DEAR JOHN,—She says I hopes he is quite well as it leaves me at present. It is raining fast. Mark Pedley's father have been caught out poaching, and have been took off to gaol. The Pedleys be a bad lot. Mark smashed my Johnnie's nose when he were at school. I reminds it well. Jane Trevaunce have jilted Mark. Come home quick. My name is Rollo, and I am writing it for her because I have nothing else to do, and because she asked me. I am a tramp, and so is my uncle. He is asleep on a sofa. I like it very much, and I never mean to go back to school any more. I must not read books. The doctor and Miss Percy says so. God bless you, my son. I hope you will come home again soon. With my best love,

"YOUR LOVING MOTHER."

"Ay, that will do first-rate, though it do sound rayther mixed," said the old woman.

"You haven't told your boy to be good like my mother in India does me," said Rollo thoughtfully. "Shall I add it in a postscript?"

"Ay, if 'tis pleasin' to 'ee. My John be a rare scholar."

So in his round, childish hand Rollo added the following: "Be a good boy, and never forget your prayers. Mother always prays that her little son may grow up a true and earnest Christian man."

"There!" said Rollo, "that is what mother put in

her last letter to me. I've copied it word for word, and now shall I put it in the envelope ? "

An envelope was produced, and after a good deal of search a stamp, and then, hearing Lionel call for him, Rollo trotted out of the kitchen feeling he had done a good afternoon's work.

He found his uncle poring over a map, and looking a little bit impatient.

"Where have you been ? Not in mischief, I hope ? We must be off at once, for it is clearing, and we are a good many miles from the village I want to reach to-night."

Rollo was only too eager to start again. The old woman came out to see them off, and entrusted the precious letter to Rollo to post. She stooped and kissed him, which brought the blood rushing to his cheeks.

"Bless your little heart. I be much oblidged to 'ee for writin' of 'un. And when 'ee cometh this way agen, I'll be vurry glad to see 'ee. Thank 'ee, master." This to Lionel, who had pressed something into her hand.

" God bless 'ee both, and send 'ee along the way safe. You'm be bravely welcome ! "

With this parting benediction the travellers went their way.

CHAPTER III

Fay, the Truant

"WHAT did you give her, uncle?"

"A shilling and a little book."

"What was the book called? Your pockets seem full of books."

Lionel looked down on the boy with a strange smile, then he said simply—

"I'm more backward with my tongue than you are. I prefer to use other people's words to my own. It was a message I wanted her to have, and I did not know how to give it myself."

"Who sent her a message? Did you know we were coming to see her?"

"I wanted to tell her that God loved her."

There was silence. This uncle seemed a strange man to Rollo, but he could not refrain from saying, "Doesn't everybody know that?"

"They don't remember it."

"And the little book told her about it?"

"Yes."

Rollo rode on, with his eyes fixed on the soft grey clouds, which were here and there disclosing the deep blue behind them.

"Don't you wish we were on the tramp to heaven?" he asked dreamily.

It was Lionel's turn to be surprised now, but he was learning to take his small nephew's strange speeches very quietly. "Well, I trust we are not tramping away from it," he said gravely.

They were again silent. On the high-road now, with the young green in the tall hedges smelling fresh and moist after the recent rain; birds busy chattering their love one to the other as they built their nests in the many trees and bushes that edged the road, and the faint lowing of cattle in the fields telling that milking time was drawing near. Gleams of sunshine pierced the thin grey clouds, and in the distance the shadows chased each other over the blue hills. Presently they met a flock of sheep, then a carrier with a couple of laughing girls on the front seat of his cart, and then a little farther on they were stopped by an anxious-faced clergyman. He looked dusty and heated, and seemed to have come some distance on foot.

"Excuse me," he said courteously, "but have you passed a little girl on the road? My small grandchild has run away, and I am looking for her."

Rollo was interested at once, and the clergyman explained with an anxious smile that the little truant had been absent since seven o'clock that morning.

"She has a trick of decamping directly she is dressed, and I don't know how to break her of it. Her mother sent her to me whilst she is on the Continent with her husband; and I suppose I don't know enough of children to have the charge of them. My old housekeeper can't manage her. This is the third time it has

happened. Once she was brought back by a farmer
eight miles off. I am afraid of what may happen to
her."

He seemed relieved to pour out his woes, and Lionel
condoled with him, offering to join him in his search.

They all turned down a lane bordered by great
overhanging banks of fern and yellow broom.

"We are runaways too," said Lionel, with a smile.
"It is a pleasant experience; so you must not be hard
on your little grandchild."

The clergyman looked at him keenly. "In search of
health, I should surmise," he said drily.

"I hope it won't be long before that statement will
be an impossible one," Lionel replied, with a short
laugh. "Yes, we have run away from town, and work,
and our fellow-creatures; and are drifting along from
day to day, living only in the present, and ignoring the
past and future."

"A dangerous experience to those in full health, but
perhaps in your case it may affect a cure."

"It is to be hoped so."

"And yet," said the clergyman thoughtfully, "I don't
know that we human beings, the products of the Eternal
God, ought ever to be in the position you describe.
Such a life is only for animals of the lower order of
creation."

"I spoke carelessly," said Lionel gravely; "the
unseen things are real to both of us."

Here Rollo broke in, for the talk was above his head.
"We are tramps, not runaways," he said, turning his big
eyes upon their new acquaintance.

"Ah well," said the clergyman, with a smiling nod,

"they are very much the same thing. I have seen a good many tramps in my time. I divide them into two classes, those who tramp because they like it, those who tramp because they are obliged. And the first class is the most numerous. I generally find they have run away from the right, from duty, principle, and honour, from honest labour, and civilisation."

" And the second class ? "

" I always help them. I probe them well first; but I have had much practice in dealing with them, and I am rarely deceived."

He talked away, but his eyes were as busy as his tongue.

Presently with the agility of a schoolboy he mounted the bank, and then with an excited wave of his hand he beckoned to Lionel to join him.

" Do you not see something white moving by that stream under the willows? There, look! What is it ? "

" A goose I should think," said Lionel.

" No geese would be wandering in these parts. Here, help me over, I believe it is the truant ! "

" Let me go for you."

" No, no, I am as active as a sailor. Wait a few minutes, and I will join you again."

Lionel gazed at him in wonder, as over brambles, hawthorn, and wire he bounded. Then once in the green meadow he set off at a quick run towards the distant stream. Lionel descended the bank and joined his little nephew in the road.

Rollo's eyes were glowing. " I wish I could get off my pony, and run away to look for her. It's like the

books say. When you travel, you always find a girl
somewhere. And then she has to be helped along,
because she is a girl."

"You have read too much," said Lionel, with a
smile.

"I wonder why she's run away," said Rollo meditatively; "p'raps the housekeeper beats her."

A shout was heard, and in a very short time the old
clergyman appeared, holding by the hand a little white-
frocked maiden in a blue cotton sunbonnet.

"There," he said triumphantly as he planted her down
in the road and looked at her with a doubtful smile.
"She is found again, and I hope this will be the last
experience of the sort."

She stood there, with rosy cheeks and golden curls, a
little fairy-like creature; one chubby finger was in her
mouth, the other hand held her shoes and stockings;
there was mischief and defiance in her eyes, though she
looked very near tears.

"Now what will you do?" she demanded of her
grandfather. He shook his head in a helpless way, and
seemed to have lost all his brisk activity.

"I can't carry you home," he said gravely, "and you
will be very, very tired before we get there."

The small finger was taken out of her mouth and
pointed at Rollo instantly.

"I'll ride on that boy's pony!"

"Yes," said Rollo in delight as he jumped down at
once, "and then I can walk. I'm tired of riding."

"Are you bound for our moorland village?" asked
the clergyman.

"We are making our way to Clugford," said Lionel.

"Oh, that is my parish. If you could give her a lift for a part of the way it would be a charity."

"But I must put my shoes and stockings on," pursued the little damsel, sitting down by the roadside, and putting her words into action with such speed, that Rollo gazed at her in amazement.

Once on the pony, her defiance melted away; and her tiny hands alternately clutched the reins and patted the pony's silky mane. Rollo, with his head erect, marched by his side holding the bridle. Their elders behind them fell into earnest conversation, the children chatted in their own irrelevant fashion.

"I was in the water when Gran found me. I was kicking frogs along ! "

"Was it nice ? "

"Yeth. I picked flowers for Gran, and then a nasty sheeps eat them all up."

"And what else did you do ? "

"I don't know."

"What's your name ? Mine is Rollo."

"I'm Fay—that's what my mummie calls me. I'm a fairy. I run away when the fairies call ; of coursth I do, and then we dance and sing, and ring the pretty blue-bells to make muthic, and I was going away in the water till I met a little boat, and then I was going to cross the big sea and find mummy ; and then we would go to the bottom of the sea and play with fishes."

"And did the fairies call you away this morning ? " asked Rollo, following this lisping maiden's words with breathless eagerness.

"Yeth ; but I want my dinner ! "

The poor little soul came down from her airy fancies

C

to plain fact. She had eaten nothing all day, beyond the slice of bread-and-butter given to her after being dressed. Rollo watched the small lips quiver and the saucy eyes get misty with coming tears. Then he hastily ransacked his pockets.

"Here's a biscuit I didn't eat, and a bullseye."

Smiles broke out at once. "Make the pony gallop. I'm tired of going slowly."

Dandy was touched with the whip; he broke into a trot, but soon relapsed into his usual walk. He was not going to hurry himself for the caprices of a small stranger. Was he not in the land of leisure? Did any native around know the meaning of haste? They came down a steep hill soon; so steep that Lionel took Rollo's place, and guided the pony carefully. As they neared the bottom the clergyman, the Rev. Antony West by name, pointed to a distant building in a nook by the riverside.

"That's an old place you ought to see—the ruins of an old monastery. A widow lady lives there, and the ruins are her great grief. She covers them up with creepers and flowers of all sorts, and refuses to admit any tourists. Her own dwelling is the pink of neatness; I am the only privileged person who is allowed free entrance. I will take you there to-morrow, if you like. I should much like to offer you both hospitality, but my housekeeper is so upset over this little one's disappearance, that household matters have come to a standstill. I dare not assure you of a hearty welcome from her."

"Which inn do you recommend?" Lionel asked a little later as they were climbing up as steep a hill as the one they came down.

"The old original one—the 'Three Feathers.' It is

exactly opposite my church, and is the oldest and most picturesque building in the place. You ask to see the visitors' book to-night. They will bring you in two ancient ledgers, one of which bears signatures in 1600."

At the top of the hill they came to the village. It was now a lovely evening; the thatched cottages, the old elms in their first spring beauty, the moor in the distance, all delighted our travellers. Perhaps Rollo was too taken up with his little playmate to be as quickly observant as usual, but when the inn was reached and a halt was made, he turned inquiringly to his uncle. "Are we going to have something to eat now?"

"Yes, I hope so," said Lionel, gazing at the grey stone building, thatched roof, and casement windows with deep interest. Mr. West drew his attention to the old stone archway which led through into the yard.

"A man was shot here by a Roundhead in the Civil Wars," said Mr. West, pointing to a niche in the wall with the indentation of the bullet plainly discernible.

Fay had dismounted and tugged her grandfather by the hand. "I'm so hungry, Gran."

"Ah, you deserve to go to bed supperless," was the quick reply; "but you know I don't train you properly. Come along. You shall see your little friend to-morrow."

They went, and Lionel and his nephew were shown into an empty coffee-room, which looked rather dreary and forlorn. However, when food was brought to them, and a fire lighted by Lionel's request, they felt quite snug and comfortable. They had it to themselves, and Rollo was full of his little companion.

"She said she was a fairy, and I believe she is," he

said to his uncle with a wise nod of his head. " I'd like
her to come with us."

" That is out of the question," said Lionel, with a
tired yawn.

" Tell you what ! " suggested Rollo, with bright eyes,
" the next chapter of our book will be about runaways."

" How will you work it out ? If you wait till we have
finished our meal, I will make a few notes."

Lionel spoke in lazy tones. Yet when they had risen
from the table he took an armchair by the fire, and proceeded to draw Rollo out for his amusement. The boy
lay on the rug, and commenced thoughtfully.

" We'll write about different runaways—tramps like us,
and boys and girls from school, and horses, and dogs,
and they all meet in the country somewhere, and have a
jolly time."

" And never come to grief ? I think most runaways
come to a bad end."

" Why do they ? Why do people think it wicked to
go off by yourself away from everybody ? "

Lionel did not answer. Rollo gazed into the fire and
wrinkled his forehead in thought. At last he glanced
up, and never did his blue eyes have a more seraphic
look as now.

" If I lived alone, I would never do a sin ! "

This astounding statement made Lionel open his
eyes.

" You little Pharisee ! Do I make you 'do sins,' as
you express it ? "

" When I'm naughty," Rollo explained slowly, " it's
generally because I do something I've been told not to ;
people always tell boys not to do so many things that

they can't remember. If I had no one to say things to me, I should get on first-rate. And there would be no one to fight or quarrel with."

"You would like to be a hermit, a recluse, who takes all the good things in life from God and his fellow-men, and never gives anything in return. You would be like a stagnant pool then, instead of a fresh running stream. I should wish you to have a nobler idea of life than that."

"Oh, when I grow up I should be different. I think if boys were let alone like grown-up people they'd be much gooder!"

"And supposing you don't live to grow up? Do you think a boy only ought to live to please himself?"

Rollo looked serious. "Shall I tell you how I'd like to live?"

"By all means."

"I should do lessons always on rainy days. Every rainy day in the year I should do lessons hard, and every fine day I should get out of doors. I should never live in London, but I would have a house in the country with a football and cricket field, and lots of boys to play with. And on Sunday I would do all the good, and think all the good that I could. I would like a governess or a mother for when I had a headache or was ill, and I would like a man like you when I wanted to travel or when I wanted to talk sense. And I think I would grow up a pretty good man, don't you?"

"A boy who has things his own way when he is young, grows up a selfish disagreeable man, and a dead failure in life," said Lionel gravely.

"I wouldn't like to be that," Rollo responded,

clasping his hands behind his head and gazing into the fire again; "but I don't want to wait to have things my own way till I grow up."

"You won't get it then. None of us ever do."

"The Runaways do," said Rollo, coming back with a child's pertinacity to the subject in hand.

"I think we'll write a chapter on 'Runaways,'" said Lionel, with his dry little smile. "We will put on the title page something of this sort—

> 'I've run away
> To get my way,
> I've lost my way to get it
> I've found the way
> To get my way
> Is not so easy, is it?'"

"I think I'll go to bed," said Rollo, with a puzzled face. "That is rather difficult to understand."

CHAPTER IV

Mrs. Duncan,
the Gardener

THE next morning our travellers were up early.
Breakfast over, they sauntered into the old
church opposite, and then made their way
down to the river, which wound like a silver streak
through moss-covered boulders of grey granite round
the little village, and away into the heart of the moor
beyond.

Mr. West joined them here, but whilst he and Lionel
sat down to have a chat on the relative merits of Devonshire and Cornwall trout-fishing, Rollo wandered away,
and soon found himself outside the ruined priory they
had been told about. With a boy's curiosity he climbed
up the old stone wall, and, perching himself on the top,
saw, to his surprise, an old lady watering her flowers.
A cotton sunbonnet was on her head, and large leather
gloves covered her hands ; her skirt was pinned up, and
her feet were encased in a huge pair of indiarubber over-
shoes. But it was not her appearance that surprised
him so much as her voice. Though no one was
apparently within hearing, she was chattering away in
a thin cracked tone, and every now and then she

would give a delighted chuckle, and laugh at her own wit.

And Rollo, listening, heard that she was not talking to herself, but to everything that came within her reach.

"Aha! my good Mr. Bumble, your feast is on my nasturtiums this morning I see! Then for goodness' sake don't tantalise my sweet peas with your near approach. They are susceptible to masculine attentions, and are simpering and fluttering with delighted anticipation of your visit.

"But as to you, Master Grub, you are not going to creep into my best La France without a protest on my side. No, if your mission this morning is to destroy, it shall be something I value less than my roses. Allow me to conduct you to the other side of the wall; you will find a good many relations creeping out in the sun—— What! Now this is the most outrageous piece of impudence!"

She had sighted Rollo, and stood looking up at him with a threatening gesture as she brandished her trowel in her hand.

Rollo was too interested to be abashed. "Oh, please go on! Where are Master Grub's relations? Is he a caterpillar? Please don't mind me. It's like a story. And please I'll be very good. I won't talk—I'll only listen."

"I have one thing that I always use upon interlopers," said the old lady severely, "and if you do not make yourself scarce this moment, I will bring it into action."

Rollo looked uneasy. "Is it a gun?" he asked.

"It is a garden hose," was the grim reply, and the old

lady rapidly walked towards that implement, that lay in many white coils upon her lawn.

Rollo saw there was determination in her action, and with a sigh he was preparing to scramble down from his post, when his foot caught in a loose stone; he tripped, and in another moment he fell with an alarming thud down on the wrong side of the wall, right into a strawberry bed.

With a shriek the old lady left her hose, and running up seized hold of him with a trembling grasp. "Are your bones broken, you rascal? Stand up and see. Your head cut? Your teeth firm? Well, it's more than you deserve! Not hurt at all?"

Rollo straightened himself manfully.

"I'm all right. I'm awfully sorry, I'll go out at the gate."

His blue eyes assumed a piteous look as he gazed up at his questioner, his lips turned a whitish blue, he put his hand to his head, and with a little murmur, "Very sorry. I only feel a—a bit queer!" he fell a little limp lifeless figure at the old lady's feet.

She gazed at him in horror; then ran into the house, and presently returned with a strong hard-featured maid in cap and apron.

"Bless your heart, mum, 'tis only a faint. I'll carry him in and bring him round in no time. He's hurt his head most likely, and had a shock. He looks as if there ain't much go in him!"

When Rollo came to his senses he found himself on an old chintz-covered couch in a cool dark room.

"Have I been asleep?" he asked dreamily.

"You've given me a nice fright," was the sharp

retort. "Yes, Bridget, I shall speak my mind if I
choose. Boys are always thoughtless, pretending to be
what they are not. Why did he say he was not hurt?
Why didn't he tell me he had a bump as big as a duck's
egg on the back of his head? Then I should have been
prepared for his collapse!"

The old lady was sitting a little distance from the
couch looking at Rollo with stern eyes. Bridget, the
maid, was standing close to him, and smiled appro-
vingly as she noted the colour stealing back to the little
white cheeks.

"You've had a tumble, laddie; where's your home?"

"I haven't got one. I'm a tramp with Uncle Lionel."
Rollo sat up as he spoke, and slid off the sofa, wondering at a bandage round his head, and still feeling rather
dazed.

"You don't look much like it," said Bridget, as she
deliberately picked him up in her strong arms and seated
him on the couch again. "Now stay there and answer
the missus's questions. I have my fowl to pick yet, and
my pudding to make."

She stalked out of the room, and a softer light came
into her mistress's eyes as she gazed at the little fellow
facing her.

"Now just sit still and give me your family history,
and don't tell me you are a tourist, for I hate
them."

Rollo did as he was told, but before his story was
done, a sharp ring at the old bell in the courtyard was
heard, and a minute afterwards Mr. West and his uncle
were ushered in.

Their surprise was great when they saw him and

heard of his accident, and Lionel was anxious at his looks.

"He's a bit of an invalid," he said to old Mrs. Duncan, "travelling for his health. His head is the weak part about him. Why couldn't you manage to injure your feet instead, Rollo? It would have been more convenient!"

Rollo looked grieved, not seeing the twinkle in his uncle's eye.

"I didn't want to manage anything," he replied, with downcast eyes.

"Except peep and pry into a private garden and give a peaceable old woman a fright," put in Mrs. Duncan. "I shall keep him here as a prisoner for the rest of the day," she added, turning to Lionel with a little defiance in her tone.

"He will be a fortunate prisoner," said Mr. West, smiling. "I know how comfortable Mrs. Duncan makes her visitors!"

"Tuts! Just leave him to me, and I'll see that his head gets into its normal condition again. Now I suppose you'll be wanting me to act showman over my own house. This is the very last time I'll do such a thing, Mr. West, even for friends of yours. I'll not encourage people making gods of mouldy beams and rotten stones and mortar. It's morbid curiosity hankering after a dead generation, that was no better or worse than our own is to-day! Did I ever tell you the story of my broken soap dish that was thrown over the wall by one of the maids? It was dug up by a tourist poking about amongst the fallen stones outside. He declared it was old English pottery of the thirteenth century, and I believe deposited it in the museum of Exeter. Now come this way. We will leave the boy here. He can't get into mischief."

They left the room, and Rollo, only conscious of a bruised and aching head, lay still in perfect content. Presently Bridget came in with a small basin of delicious-smelling soup.

"Ye'll need something to pull you round after your tumble," she said. "The mistress will see that you don't want, I can tell you."

Rollo sat up and gratefully consumed every drop.

"I shall have to be going on soon," he said gravely. "Is the sun very hot just now?"

"Ay! isn't it?"

And Bridget pulled up the venetian blind to let him see the sunny garden with the simmering heat rising from the ground.

"No laddie," she went on. "You must have a quiet day now. Would you like a picture book?"

"No thank you. I think I'll—I'll lie still. I feel Dandy will joggle me dreadfully. Do you think uncle would wait till to-morrow to go on?"

"We will ask him. Bide you there now, like a good little man."

Bridget disappeared, and the cool and stillness of the darkened room had such a soothing effect, that before very long Rollo was fast asleep. He was roused at last by voices.

"Leave him here, Mr. Derrick. If you want to do the neighbourhood, do it, and come back for him to-morrow. He doesn't look fit for anything. I'll feed him up, and keep him quiet. The question is not so

much, if he will like it, as whether it will be good for
him, and I'll answer for it that a sick child is the better
for a woman's nursing and care."

"You are right, Mrs. Duncan."

"It is very kind of you, but I hardly like——"

"What is it?" asked Rollo suddenly.

Then Lionel bent over him.

"Look here, little chap, this kind lady wants to keep
you here till to-morrow and look after you. Will you
stay with her? You seem rather shaky, and it will
give Dandy a good rest if you do. How do you
feel?"

"I've only—only a bit of a headache," murmured
Rollo, looking from one face to the other in a little
bewilderment.

Then he held out his small hand to Mrs. Duncan.

"I think," he said slowly, "I like women best when
I've a headache—I'll stay, please."

They laughed, and Lionel said as he was departing,
"He knows when he is well off."

Then Rollo dozed off to sleep again, and only woke
to receive a dainty little lunch brought to his couch
on a tray.

But in the afternoon he felt better. Mrs. Duncan
brought some knitting in and sat in an easy chair by the
window, and they soon drifted into talk.

"I should like to live with you for a little," Rollo
announced. "I've never lived in a garden. There's a
good deal to see, I should think."

"So there is everywhere, if we use our eyes."

"Yes, but in London where I live, you get tired of the
people. There are hardly any animals. Only horses

and cats and dogs. And no flowers and fruit growing.
They are all picked before you get them."

"I hardly think they would be growing anywhere long
if you were about," was the dry retort.

"Well, it's half the fun picking, isn't it? But I like
to see them growing too. And then there are wild
animals in the country—the rabbits, and squirrels, and
hares, and the bees, and butterflies, and all the birds!
I didn't know such birds were made till I saw them.
Uncle tells me their names. It's a pity the people in
London leave no room for animals, or for the country
things."

"It is a pity indeed," assented Mrs. Duncan.

Then Rollo came to more personal matters. "Have
you ever had any boys or girls live with you?"

"Never."

"Did you never play with any when you were a little
girl?"

Mrs. Duncan looked at him with tightening lips.

"I was born after my father's death," she said, "and
my mother died when I was a fortnight old. I was
brought up by my aunt, who disliked children, and my
childhood was one long martyrdom. She and a
governess effectually crushed all joy that might have
been my portion. My husband was chosen for me. He
was twice my age and a confirmed invalid. It was a
nurse he needed, not a wife. I don't know why I am
telling you this, but mine has been an unloved life from
the beginning. I never played as a child, I never
enjoyed life when I was young. When my husband died
I took this old house, and my latter days are better than
the beginning."

"That's like Job," said Rollo, a sparkle coming in his eyes. "I'm very fond of poor Job. I like to read about him. It says that God blessed the latter end of him more than the beginning."

"I cannot say I have had much blessing," said Mrs. Duncan, with a queer little laugh. "An unloved and unloving creature I am, and I am content to be so."

Rollo looked a little puzzled. "I like people to like me, but I think only mother loves me and—God."

There was silence. Then the boy added reflectively, "There's God left to love you."

Mrs. Duncan gave a kind of grunt, and Rollo, pursuing his thoughts aloud, as was his custom, continued—

"Uncle wanted to tell a woman that, and he gave her a little book about it. I expect you know it without any telling. I thought everybody did, but Uncle said they didn't remember it."

"Is your uncle a parson? He didn't look like it."

"Oh, no. He is just a tramp, he says."

They drifted then into talk over the garden, and once on her hobby Mrs. Duncan had much to say to her interested and breathless listener.

As the afternoon shadows began to creep across the sunny garden, Bridget made her appearance once more.

"I've taken the tea into the garden, ma'am, under the beech-tree. Shall I carry the little gentleman out, or will he walk?"

"Oh, I can walk," said Rollo hastily.

Tea on the lawn under the shady beech was delicious. Rollo was conscious of the restfulness of the scene, and Mrs. Duncan seemed to have lost her sharp abruptness.

Since describing her beloved flowers, her voice had
become almost soft in tone.   Very soon after it was
over he was taken indoors again, and put to bed in a
dainty little room by old Bridget; and in spite of an
aching head Rollo was soon fast asleep.

CHAPTER V

Stranded

ROLLO was quite well enough the next day to continue his travels, and after bidding his old hostess a warm farewell, he found himself again jogging along through the fresh leafy lanes with his uncle.

He gave a very full account of his visit to Lionel, who listened for the most part in silence.

"The latter end of my visit was better than the beginning," concluded Rollo quaintly. "I suppose ends often are."

"Ends are pretty much what we make them," said Lionel.

"But no one wants to make a bad end to anything," argued the child.

"They make a bad beginning, and the end follows suit."

"Then I ought to have had a bad end yesterday."

"Yes, you were mercifully preserved from your deserts."

"The biggest end of all is heaven," said the boy dreamily.

"We are told of another," was the quiet response.

There was silence. The sunshine and life around

them led to lighter subjects. Up and down hill, over a
wild bit of moor where the rabbits scampered about in
hundreds, then into a woodland glade on the side of a
hill, and all this time they had not met a human being.
It was cool and shady under the old beeches that
bordered their way, and when they got into the depths
of a mossy dell with last year's copper leaves still
carpeting the ground, and the grand old trees just
meeting above their heads, Lionel took off his hat, and
with bare head stood up to meet the gentle breeze that
fanned his heated brow.

" We must have a halt here ; it will be good for our
minds and bodies," he said.

" Yes," assented Rollo, slipping off his pony ; "and
I'm quite hungry for some dinner."

Dandy was tethered to a tree in an open space near
where he could munch some soft grass to his great satisfaction. Then Lionel began to unpack his knapsack.
He was a good caterer, and Rollo looked on with
pleased eyes as a bottle of milk, rolls, hard-boiled eggs,
cheese, and buns were all deposited on the ground.

" Now I tell you what we will do," said Lionel ; "we
will be two old women to-day, and have a good cup of
tea. I've got a packet here. You get some sticks
together and we'll make a fire."

Away darted Rollo. This was after his own heart.
Sticks and dry leaves soon made a cheery blaze. Lionel
filled his tin mug with water from the stream, and set it
on the fire to boil. And a few minutes after they were
both enjoying a cup of tea, far more refreshing under
the circumstances, than it would have been in any lady's
drawing-room.

Rollo ate heartily; then when he had finished his meal, sat watching the fire with fascinated gaze, whilst Lionel took out his pipe, and pulling his hat over his eyes, prepared for a siesta.

"I've been thinking——" began Rollo.

"Go on thinking," interrupted Lionel lazily; "but let me think too, and leave me alone for an hour."

Rollo got up and cheerfully obeyed. He climbed trees, he broke rotten branches, he found a chaffinch's nest, he watched two stoats' perambulations, he revelled in his surroundings, and longed that he could be a woodcutter and have his home in a wood. The afternoon sun crept through the trees, and still Lionel lay like a lotus-eater on his mossy couch.

At last his call, ringing through the wood, startled the birds and rabbits, and brought Rollo breathless and panting to his side.

"We must hurry on. I have been asleep, and did not notice the time. We are a good ten miles from where I want to put up to-night."

"I should like to stay here years," said Rollo, as he mounted Dandy's back, and looked wistfully through the green arches and brown glades. "It seems wasted if no one is here."

Lionel smiled. "God has many corners of His beautiful earth that are still unspoilt by man's presence."

Rollo pondered over this, then he said humbly, "I'm afraid I've spoilt a little of it this afternoon. I stripped some bark off a tree, and broke three branches, and dug up some moss."

Lionel was about to make some reply when a sound behind him made him look round. There, with the low sunlight on her curly head, and her white sunbonnet dangling by one string in her hand, came little Fay. She stepped up to them serenely.

"I've been coming after you all day. I want to be a tramp."

Lionel stood astounded. "How on earth have you followed us?" he asked.

Fay's radiant face became slightly clouded. "You're cross!" she pouted. "I've been running and walking and sitting in a cart a part of the way, for I got in when they wasn't looking, and I gotted out when they stopped. I followed Dandy's feet in the mud."

Rollo got down from his pony with shining eyes. His little soul was moved by Fay's enterprising spirit. He moved towards her admiringly. "You're splendid!" he said. "Oh, uncle, let her tramp with us; she's every bit as good as a boy!"

But Lionel looked vexed beyond measure, and did not view the little runaway with as much delight as his nephew.

"You're a very naughty little girl," he said sternly; "and if I were your grandfather I would lock you in a room all day, or hobble you, as they do the donkeys."

"I'm coming with you," repeated Fay, with an obstinate turn to her small mouth. "I like the boy, and if he rides Dandy and has picnics every day, I shall do it too!"

Lionel rubbed his head in perplexity.

"You won't send her back?" pleaded Rollo coaxingly.

"I shall have to take her back this moment on the

pony," was Lionel's reply. "I hope I shall meet some one on the way coming after her. It is too bad to hinder us so."

Rollo looked subdued at once. "Must we go back?"

"You mustn't. You could never walk it. Now look here, Rollo, can I trust you?"

With those fearless blue eyes fastened on him, Lionel spoke more gently.

"You must walk on steadily by yourself till you come to the next village. I will put you in the road, and you can't make a mistake. It is only two miles and a half. Duneven it is called. You must go to the little inn, and wait there till I come. You have not done much walking to-day, so I think you will manage it. We must give up the idea of getting on farther to-day."

Rollo held up his head importantly. "Of course I can manage it. I could walk six miles easy!"

"You must wait at Duneven till I come. Now, young lady, up you get! I wonder what will cure you from playing these pranks?"

Fay indignantly protested against being taken home. Finding Lionel in earnest, she burst into floods of tears, and it needed Rollo to comfort her.

"Don't cry, Fay; when I grow up to be a man I will find you out, and will marry you, and then we will ride through woods all the summer and live in castles in the winter. Won't you like that?"

Fay dried her tears at once.

"And will you let me live *alwayth* out of doors?"

"Always."

Then she threw her arms round his neck and kissed

him. "I'll *never* forget it," she said; "and mind you
bring plenty of buns with you!"

Then quite cheerfully she allowed herself to be seated
on Dandy, who was started at a trot, and waving a farewell to Rollo, she called out—

"You must knock at the door three knocks, and I'll
know who you are!"

Lionel walked at her side, after giving his small
nephew final directions, and murmured under his breath.
" The ways of children are passing strange."

Rollo tramped along sturdily for some time. After
the wood the road did not appear very interesting; it
was bordered by high banks and hedges, and when
curiosity impelled him to mount to the top he only saw
fields stretching away on each side.

Elation at tramping along alone kept up his spirits
for a time. He whistled and sang; he longed that his
little London schoolfellows could see him in this strange
country, and then he began to wish he had some one to
whom he could talk.

"If only uncle had let Fay come with us! I do want
some one that really can understand things. I'll marry
her when I grow up, and we'll have two ponies; hers
will be white, and mine black, and we'll have no one to
tell us where to go and when to stop. I wonder when
I shall see Fay again, and I wonder where she'll run
away to next? I expect she'd like to be me. I shall
go into the inn, and ask for supper to be got ready
like uncle does. Oh dear, this is a very long road!
I wish some one would come along!"

But no one came, and Rollo's short legs began to ache.
" It's quite ten miles, I'm sure; I've walked for ever so

many hours, and it's nothing but a road for ever and
ever ! "

At last some cottages were to be seen, and the little
fellow quickened his pace.

Then came a blacksmith's shop, and there Rollo had
to stop, for the fascination of it proved too much for him.
A horse was being shod, and he watched the process
from beginning to end.   Never in London had he been
so favoured.   Another boy was watching too, and the
two interchanged a few remarks.

As Rollo turned away, the village boy followed him.
"Where be 'ee goin'? "

"To the inn," was the prompt reply, "where is it? "
A rather dirty forefinger indicated a small white house
with a creaking signboard, that was swaying to and fro in
the evening breeze.

" Where do 'ee come from; not these parts? " the
rustic continued.

Rollo gave his usual answer with cheerfulness.

" I'm a tramp, and my uncle is behind, and I'm to
wait for him at the inn."

" Got any coppers? "

" I have two—three I think," said Rollo grandly,
jingling some loose coin in his packet.

"Gi' me one for tellin' 'ee the inn."

" But," objected Rollo, "you don't want a penny
because I asked you the way."

The village boy grinned, then with a change of tone
he said; "Want ter see a live fox? "

" Oh, where? "

" A'll show 'ee the nest of 'un through that 'ere gate."

It was a bait that took.   Rollo eagerly followed him

through into a field. A moment later he was tripped up, his pocket rifled of the few coin he possessed, and the village lad was out of sight. Rollo picked himself up, a wiser and a sadder boy. He came in a few minutes to the inn, and looked up disconsolately at the signboard. It represented a bull's head of ferocious aspect with bloodshot eyes, and frothy lips, the tongue hanging out, and horns lowered ready for a charge.

Rollo turned away his eyes, and walked in at the old doorway. There were three or four men seated in the small tap-room with mugs of beer, and they were too busy with their talk to notice him. But lounging against the door was the landlord, and as he smoked his pipe with a pleasant smile, Rollo addressed him timidly.

"Please is this the inn?"

"Yes, the 'Black Bull,' established since 1700 or thereabouts."

"Can't I wait here? My uncle is coming on, and he told me to come here first. I expect we shall like some supper."

"Here, wife!" the landlord shouted; "see to this young gentleman; let him wait in the parlour."

Out came a gentle-faced, careworn-looking woman, who took him into a very fusty little parlour with a stale smell of tobacco and of spirits. The window was blocked with geraniums and fuchsias. Rollo looked round it with a sinking heart.

"May I have a glass of milk?" he asked. "I'm so thirsty. I s'pose my uncle won't be very long."

"I'll bring you a glass of milk, if you set still, and promise not to get into mischief," was the gloomy reply.

Rollo seated himself in a high chair, and swinging his

legs surveyed the room. There were a few highly-coloured sporting prints on the walls, some books on a glass chiffonier, and a wonderful array of china on a shelf above his head.

" There's no mischief that I could do," was his thought. " I wish uncle would come."

He had his milk, and then patiently sat and waited. The sun was setting now, and the room began to get dusk. At last his patience was exhausted. He opened the door and went out. The landlord was still standing by the door, but a man passing by had stopped for a chat, and their tongues were almost as busy as those in the tap-room. Rollo stood and listened. At last the man in the street went on, and the boy ventured a remark.

" How many people do you talk to in a day? "

The landlord looked at him with a twinkle in his eye

" All the world," he said, " leastways all *my* world."

" There are lots of worlds, aren't there ? " said Rollo, in his meditative fashion. " I have two, and one of them is quite a little old world to me now. It's London, and my school there. Would you like me to tell you about it ? "

Rollo's silent time in the stuffy little parlour had brought him out panting to talk to some one. The landlord looked him down, and seeing possible entertainment for himself in this small, large-eyed, white-faced boy, seated himself on the wooden bench outside the door, and Rollo eagerly followed suit.

" I sometimes think I'd like to write a book," he continued, " and put my two worlds in it. I would have one chapter for my little world, London, and twenty

chapters for my country world. My London world is
full of noise and crowds, and lessons in a schoolroom,
and shops, and every day the same except in the holi-
days when we see a pantomime or go to Madame
Tussaud's or the Crystal Palace, but my country world—
ah!" Here the little speaker lifted his head up with a
long-drawn breath. "Oh, isn't it a lovely place?
There's something fresh every day, and there's such a
big sky, and so much room to move, and such lovely
animals and birds to see!"

"Ay, there's a powerful lot of room," said the landlord, taking his pipe out of his mouth and refilling it
slowly; "but folks mostly thinks London the big world
I reckon. My wife's nephew, he's a Londoner, and he
comes down to us and turns his nose up at our country
habits. A lively young spark he is, who has a tongue
like a baby's rattle, but he can't sit a horse square and
fair for all his London teachin', and as to drivin'—well,
he's a caution, and then he says horses be too slow nowadays, we move by steam and wheels, and he tears up
and down our roads here with his cycle, and comes in
a ragin' at our stones and ruts, till my wife, who can't
say bo to a goose, she hits out that if he'd give us notice
nex' time, we'd board our roads and carpet them for
him and his cycle! Ha! ha! When my wife does
make a joke, 'tis sure to be a good 'un!"

They talked on in the dusky twilight. Rollo gave
his experiences as a "tramp," and the landlord proved a
good listener. But when the dusk deepened into dark-
ness, and no uncle appeared, Rollo grew uneasy.

CHAPTER VI

Bobby, the
Doctor's Son

"HOW much does a bed cost?" Rollo asked presently, adding hurriedly, "I'm afraid I haven't any money at all now; a strange boy picked my pocket; I wish my uncle would come."

"Oh, well," said the landlord, Tom Bentley by name, "we won't make a trouble over that; the wife will find you a bed, and a supper too, as far as that goes. I'll give her a call!"

His voice rang out lustily, and Mrs. Bentley appeared immediately. She did not look pleased at the prospect of having Rollo as a guest, and eyed him in a discontented fashion.

"You haven't bin and run away from school, have you?" she said; "you be too small to be wanderin' about like this. Boys are all alike, and they never speak the truth, so 'tis quite impossible to pay notice to what they says. And Tom, you're that innocent, you'd take a thief in and make him comfortable. I mind that nice-spoken lad a year gone, who had a wonderful tale about his pocket bein' picked, and he had supper and a bed and a hearty breakfast, and vowed he'd call agin and pay. He never has yet, and I have a bill o' six or seven shillings for him to settle when he comes?"

Rollo's cheeks were hot and red.

"I think," he said, squaring his shoulders, and trying to look an inch taller than he really was—"I think I'll just go a little way along the road and meet my uncle."

Then he marched away with a very brave exterior, and a sinking heart.

The village seemed deserted now, lights were to be seen from the cottage windows, but the high-road lay dark and still, just discernible by the light of the rising moon.

Rollo pursed up his lips, and began to whistle.

"I am getting a bit shaky, but I won't be," he was thinking. "I won't go near that nasty woman again. I wonder what real tramps do when they have no money! I believe they go to the workhouse. I wonder if there is one here! But then uncle would never find me! I've read of boys sleeping in woods, but there only seems the road here. I do feel so awfully hungry. I don't know what to do."

Poor little Rollo! He struggled with his fears, with his loneliness and hunger; but at last tears rose to his eyes and a lump in his throat.

He walked along slowly. There was no sound or sight of any one, and then suddenly a light flashed out in front of him, and a bell sounding told him that a bicycle was coming towards him.

Then, in desperation, he called out—

"Please stop; I want to ask you something."

"Hey! What? Who on earth are you?" It was a broad-shouldered, burly figure that sprang off the bicycle, and for an instant Rollo shrank back. But the voice was that of a gentleman, and he took courage.

"I'm waiting for my uncle. Have you seen him on this road? I don't think he'll ever come, and I don't know where to sleep to-night, because I've no money."

"What is your uncle like, little man?"

"He's just like himself; he's like no one else that I can think of. He has my pony with him."

"A brown moor pony? Ah, then, I have seen him. It had cast a shoe, and he was at the blacksmith's with it, but miles away from here!"

The stranger and Rollo looked each other up and down. Then Rollo said, with a little quiver in his voice, "Can you tell me the way to the workhouse?"

"Ay, I could," said the stranger, "but I fancy I had best house you for the night. Can you step out for half a mile? I've a little son your size; he'll lay hands on you with joy."

"Please, are you the clergyman?"

"No; the other chap that you generally find in these benighted parts. Can't you guess? I look after the good folks' bodies and the parson after their souls. We halve the parishioners between us."

"But," said Rollo, standing up in the middle of the road and prepared to argue the matter out, "I shouldn't like to be halved, because my soul is me, and my body, too. I shouldn't like two people looking after me."

"Suppose you were very ill, who would you want to see?"

"My mother," promptly answered Rollo.

The doctor laughed heartily.

"I think we'll be moving on and continue our talk as we go!"

"But how will uncle know where to find me?"

"Where did he expect to find you?"

"At the inn. And I've been waiting there, but the woman wouldn't believe me, and didn't want to give me a bed."

"Mary Bentley is a skinflint. Trouble has turned her sour. Come along, and I'll leave a message with her for your uncle as we go by."

Rollo trotted along quite contentedly, but he asked presently—

"What kind of trouble has turned her sour?"

"She lost her only little girl. A mad dog bit her, and it was too late to save her. She was just bound up in that child, and has never been the same since."

Rollo wanted to hear all particulars.

"She's a person, perhaps, who would like uncle's message."

"What's that?"

"Well, it's a kind of private message, but he left a book about it with a woman we saw once. It was to tell her that God loved her."

"Is your uncle a parson?"

"No, he's just a tramp."

"He's monopolising a parson's vocation," said the doctor, with a shake of his head.

They relapsed into silence, and soon came to the "Black Bull." The doctor was evidently great friends with the landlord, for he stayed chatting to him for a good ten minutes, and Rollo waited at a discreet distance. He could not forgive the landlord's wife for taking him for a runaway schoolboy, and was thankful when the doctor joined him, and they tramped up a steep lane, arriving at a comfortable square red brick house at the top of it.

The doctor opened the door with a cheery whistle, and the next minute a rosy-faced, laughing boy came bounding down the stairs.

"Here, Bobby, come and make friends with this youngster. He is going to stay with us to-night. Tell Mrs. Crane to make him up a bed in your room. And let us have supper at once, for he is starving and so am I!"

It seemed like a pleasant dream to Rollo to be sitting down presently to a comfortable meal, and listening to the incessant chatter of Bobby. He was tired enough to like to listen instead of talk, but when the meal was over, and the doctor left, the two boys together, confidences became mutual.

"It must be a lark to go tramping along every day to different places. I wish I could come with you. I do lessons with our vicar, but I have always done them by the afternoon. Where are you going to-morrow?"

"I don't know," responded Rollo. "That's just the best of it, I never know what will turn up. I don't even know if my uncle will turn up. I hope he will."

"It's awfully late—past ten o'clock. Dad will be packing me off to bed. Look here, if I call you at five o'clock will you come out fishing with me before breakfast?"

"How do you do it? Is it hard?"

Bobby's laughter rang out. "You wait and see me! I'm a regular dab. Dad has taught me, and I know a lovely spot for trout. You ought to catch fish every morning for breakfast!"

"I thought," murmured the town boy, "that fish came out of the sea. Can you catch them in any water?"

"Where have you lived all your life?" said Bobby, with supreme contempt.

"Oh, I know I don't know anything. I've been in London, and people who live there are never taught anything at all—at least, not about the country, and all the really interesting things you ought to know."

A sharp ring at the door interrupted this conversation. It proved to be Lionel. Rollo heaved a deep sigh of relief when he saw him.

"I see you have fallen into good hands," Lionel said. "Did you think I had failed you?"

"I didn't know what to think till I met the doctor, but it's all right now," responded Rollo in a comfortable tone; "and Bobby is going to take me out to fish to-morrow morning early."

The doctor appeared, and was soon engaged in an animated discussion with Lionel, pressing him to make his house his headquarters, and insisting upon putting him up for the night.

Lionel at first refused, then demurred, and then acquiesced, for he felt it would be difficult to get away from the hospitable doctor.

Rollo was too sleepy by this time to care much what became of his uncle, and he tumbled into bed, and was sound asleep, before the doctor's housekeeper came in to see if he were comfortable.

At half-past five the next morning two small boys

were trotting across green sweet smiling meadows. Rollo lifted up his little head in ecstasy.

"Oh, how fresh and cool it is ! What is it smells so nice ? "

" It's just the early morning. It's the best time of day to be out, isn't it, when nothing has got stale and hot ? "

"Why, they're cutting hay, that's what I smell ! Oh, do let me see a hayfield ! I've never been in any, except in books."

Rollo was peering over a hedge as he spoke, but Bobby pulled him by the jacket impatiently.

"Oh, come on ! We can go into a hayfield any time of day. We shall get no fish if we don't make haste."

So Rollo was hurried on through the meadows, and down a steep bank to a clear sparkling grey stream, rushing with white foam over dark brown rocks, and shaded on both sides by overhanging trees and elder bushes. " Now keep quiet. Father says, 'Tongue still, hand steady, eye busy !' Come down here and sit on that rock. Now see me cast my line ! "

Bobby was in his own eyes the hero of the hour, but much as Rollo admired his dexterity in handling his rod, his rigid pose as a keen fisherman, and his non-chalance concerning his surroundings, the fascination of this trout river held him spellbound. No boy can resist the enthralling power of a piece of water at any time, and to Rollo this merry, dashing stream, alive with an infinity of beautiful creatures below and above its surface, with the morning sun touching it here and there with golden ripples, and with the still, dark pools

E

between the brown rocks, seemed the most delightful spot he had yet seen on his travels.

He did not want to talk, and if his eyes were busy his thoughts were busier still.

Grand excitement ensued when Bobby caught and landed his first trout. It was a small speckled one, and Rollo watched its dying struggles with pity and concern.

"It seems so cruel on such a lovely morning. He didn't think when he woke up a few hours ago that this was going to be his death morning!"

Bobby laughed. "Oh, you are a rum chap! Fishes have no feelings!"

"How do you know? I'll turn my back, if you don't mind, while the next one dies. They take such a long time doing it!"

An hour passed. The two boys had shifted their positions several times, and Bobby had caught six trout. One he declared to be two pounds, and as Rollo was ignorant on such a point, Bobby's statement was undisputed. When Bobby wound up his lines and shouldered his basket, Rollo's tongue was loosed.

"I should like to live by a river all the days of my life."

"Oh no, you wouldn't. It's awfully sticky in the middle of the day—the flies bother so. I like it before breakfast and late in the evening."

"But I shouldn't mind the flies. I like watching them, there are so many sorts. I think I should make a collection of them."

"But you wouldn't like to see them die!" said Bobby sarcastically.

"I think small things aren't so bad as big, are they?

I daresay if I saw you catch fish every morning I should get accustomed to them."

"Hush!" said Bobby, pulling hold of Rollo's coat and bringing him to a standstill. "Look at that lazy fellow on that stone there. Keep quiet, and you'll see that tiny bird feed him. It's a cuckoo. Ever seen one have his breakfast?"

"No, never!"

Rollo's eyes grew big with excitement. "Can't he get his own breakfast?"

"Hush! you'll scare them away. He's a lazy beggar, and the little bird looks after him all day. See him rolling his eye round after him, and squeaking as if he were just born? I wonder whether the tiny bird worships him or hates him? There! He's found a worm. Now look."

The cuckoo perched on a stone was opening his huge mouth, and the little bird flying up deftly dropped a worm in. Then they flew away together to repeat the exploit in the next field."

"I wonder," said Rollo thoughtfully, "which is the happy one of those birds?"

Bobby laughed. "The cuckoo, of course. He has a jolly easy time. He is born a bully, and bullies till he dies."

"But bullies are horrid. We had one at our school; he was the biggest. Miss Percy said he was too big for her. I'm sure he was too big for me. I couldn't lick him, you see, so he did what he liked with me. He went to another school last term. We were so glad. But are you sure the cuckoo is a bully? He mayn't be. Do they all make small birds feed them, or is it only the old ones and the ill ones who have them, do you think ? "

"Oh no : it's the lot of them. If you see a cuckoo flying, the little bird is always behind him."

"Little things can help big things," said Rollo thoughtfully.

Philosophy was not one of Bobby's characteristics. He burst into an animated account of an otter hunt at which he had been present, and Rollo grew keen and eager at his description. They came into the house with glowing cheeks and ravenous appetites.

Rollo found his uncle accepting his host's invitation to stay with him over the Sunday, which was the following day.

"I am a busy man myself," said the good doctor, "but my boy will introduce you to the best spot for trout fishing in the county. If you're a keen fisherman you'll take your lunch and spend the day out. I sha'n't expect you back till the evening. What do you say ? "

"That will suit me first-rate. If I am not skilful with my line I shall be laying up stores of good air and sunshine. And my small nephew revels in an open-air life."

So it was settled, and an hour afterwards Lionel and the two boys were sauntering through green meadows by the side of overhanging woods, while at their feet the grey water was dashing merrily along over rocks and boulders inviting them to sound its depth, and take from its bosom some of its numerous family.

CHAPTER VII

Sunday's
Sermon

IT was an ideal day for fishing; grey clouds swept the sky; there was a feeling of rain in the air though none actually descended. The cool breeze from the water kept the flies from being over-troublesome, and Lionel gave himself up to the pleasures of the hour. Bobby and Rollo scoured the woods, and their confidences were many and quaint.

"I hate books," said Bobby, "can't think why we need have them at all. A lot of stupid chaps who like to see their writing printed, that's all they are."

Rollo gasped.

"But I love them, they tell you such a lot!"

"My father tells me more than any book, and I can remember what he says, which is more than I do when I have to read it!"

"But if your father had never read books, he wouldn't be able to tell you anything," argued Rollo.

"Bosh! He keeps his eyes and ears open, and so do I. Books ought to be only for the deaf and dumb and blind."

"And don't you like stories?" asked Rollo, after a

pause, in which he had been trying to take in Bobby's last statement.

"Don't I just! You should hear father tell a yarn; he makes your eyes drop out of your head!"

"But," said Rollo, a little triumphantly, "s'posing you were miles away from your father, and not near anybody who could tell you stories and things, then what would you do without books?"

"I'd have a ripping good time. I'd be a Robinson Crusoe."

"But he had books, hadn't he? The Bible, you know. Oh, Bobby, you couldn't get on without the Bible."

"Why not?"

"It—it helps us to be good and teaches us about God."

"Don't you be a prig! I know all about God that I want to know."

Rollo looked embarrassed. "I don't want to be a prig, but long ago people were burnt alive because they found they couldn't live without the Bible."

Bobby was silent for a minute. "Well, p'raps I'll have the Bible for Sundays; not a single other book."

Here their conversation ended, for they came across a small group of boys round a tree. A very tiny boy was climbing with great difficulty up the topmost branches of a young elm. A bird's nest was his goal, but the light branches were swaying with his weight, and he was looking down with a scared, terrified face. "I can't go no further," he hailed, "I dursn't. I'm falling."

"You don't come down till you get it!" shouted a big boy at the foot of the tree. "I'll make 'ee climb!"

He seized a big stone and hurled it with such an accurate aim that it caught the child on the side of his head, and he uttered a sharp cry of pain.

This was too much for Rollo. The blood rushed to his face. Stepping up he confronted the bully boldly.

"What are you making him climb for when he doesn't want to, and hitting him when he can't hit back? You just stop it!"

The big boy turned in astonishment, and Rollo then recognised him as the one who had robbed him of his last pence the day before.

"Look 'ee here," he said savagely, "you make yerself scarce, or I'll send you up another tree. Small fry like you can't afford to cheek your elders."

Then Bobby came forward. "Joe Masters, you're a bully and a coward. If you aren't, take off your coat and fight me!"

There was a murmur of approval from the other small boys assembled, but Joe turned away sullenly.

"I dessay! And have the doctor after me for smashin' up his baby. No thank'ee! Not if I know it!"

Rollo looked after him in disgust as he slunk away.

"He's a thief, too, he picked my pockets yesterday."

The small boy quickly descended the tree. He was shaking from fright, and his companions who had been laughing at his plight a few moments before, now were loud in declamation against his persecutor.

"He wanted the nest and was feared to go himself, so he sent Tommy."

"He switched his legs with a stick to make him climb quicker!"

"I'll lick him well if he doesn't keep out of my sight,"

said Bobby wrathfully. "Go home, Tommy, as fast as you can, and if he touches you he'll have to reckon with me. Here! P'raps I'd better see you out of the wood. Come along."

The boys dispersed. Rollo found his way back to his uncle. He lay down on the grass by his side and watched the flowing river.

"It's a pity," he announced presently with a sigh, "that some people have to be bigger than others. They wouldn't be cruel if they were all the same size."

Lionel waited for his nephew to explain himself, and Rollo added after further thought, "There was the cuckoo this morning making the little bird feed it, and Joe making Tommy nearly kill himself to get him a bird's nest, and—and——"

"Yes?" said Lionel encouragingly.

"And you killing fishes!" finished Rollo.

Lionel smiled.

"The big species preying on the small," he remarked; "it's one of nature's laws."

There was a long silence.

"I s'pose," said Rollo slowly, "God is the only person that is quite, quite fair. I expect He thinks a beetle quite as good as a lion, and a little boy as good as a big one."

"Yes, He is quite fair," his uncle replied. "And He will be quite fair through all eternity, though atoms of the universe try to pick His character to pieces, and settle what He must do, and what He must not."

This was one of his uncle's grown-up speeches that made Rollo "ache trying to understand it," as he expressed it.

"And God loves everybody and everything," Rollo continued, with a pensive glance at some dead trout in his uncle's basket.

"You will never be a sportsman," Lionel said good-humouredly. "Give your brain a rest. I'm not in a mood to talk philosophy to-day."

"I shall have a chapter about bullies in our book," went on Rollo. "I shall put in the cuckoo, and Joe."

"Not me, I hope?"

"No, you aren't a bully," said Rollo quietly. "I'm glad we aren't all the same size for some things. What's the opposite word to bully?"

"Benefactor—will that do?"

"Yes, I shall call the chapter Bullies and Benefactors, and all big people must be one or the other."

Lionel shook his head doubtfully.

"Only two classes gives me such a poor chance. If I'm not a bully must I be a benefactor?"

"Yes," said Rollo firmly. "I'm not quite sure what a benefactor is, but it's something good, and the very opposite to Joe and the cuckoo."

"I will try to be it," murmured Lionel, with a twinkle in his eye.

"Fancy!" said Rollo incredulously, "Bobby hates books. He just hates them and says they're no good at all."

"He's a little savage!"

"He says they're only made for deaf and dumb and blind people."

"He's a little fool."

"He knows more than I do, though. He says he

gets it all from his father. But his father can't be quite as good as a library of books, can he ? "

Lionel shook his head.

" Do you think, to-morrow being Sunday, and there being a good many books in the doctor's study, and possibly raining, I might just read one of them ? "

" I think you had better not. I promised your governess you should not open one."

" Except the Bible," said Rollo. " I've got that, you know, in my bag."

" Yes, I will allow you that."

Bobby appeared at this minute very red and breathless.

" Time for lunch," he announced. " I've seen those small boys to the village, and given Joe Masters a bit of my mind."

Rollo delightedly helped to unpack the luncheon from the basket, and in a few minutes fisherman and boys were contentedly munching their sandwiches and meat pies. Bobby was the talker, Lionel lay back against a granite boulder, and save when he put in a word or two, seemed wrapped in thought.

" I wish you'd stay a good long time with us," said Bobby, " we'd have ripping fun ! or, better still, couldn't you take me on with you ? Dad would let me go. I'm sure you want some chap to keep you lively, don't you?"

" Not I ! " said Lionel, when he was appealed to. " I'm a quiet peaceable individual, and Rollo and I know each other's ways by this time. I couldn't take charge of another boy."

" A little girl wanted to join us yesterday," said Rollo. " It would be rather fun to gather a company together

as we went along the road. It would be like the Canter-
bury pilgrims."

" Who are they ? " asked Bobby.

" Oh, they are book people. You wouldn't like them.
I have pictures of them in London."

" I shouldn't like to be mixed up with girls," said
Bobby, with fine scorn.

" And I am not going to have a dozen imps tied to
my tail, I assure you," asserted Lionel.

They finished their lunch; then the two boys disappeared, and the joys of that afternoon's scramble in
the woods by the river dwelt long in Rollo's memory.

He was a very tired but a very happy boy as he walked
into the house that evening, and when Lionel went to
see him the last thing before he retired for the night, he
heard him drowsily murmuring to himself: "There are
bullies and benefactors, and Bobby and birds, but they're
all beautiful—and I love the world in the woods ! "

Sunday dawned fair and cloudless. Lionel took the
two boys to the parish church ; the doctor was away on
his rounds. There was a hush and stillness in the little
country church that was very restful to Lionel Derrick's
spirit. The vicar, an old grey-haired man, preached
from the text, " Who died for us, that whether we wake
or sleep we should live together with Him."

Lionel listened, and thought. He stepped out of
church with a glow in his eyes that told of the quickening of his soul. Rollo walked beside him with knitted
brow, Bobby danced here and there, delighted that the
long service was over. The doctor was home to early
dinner, but he was called to a patient immediately afterwards. Lionel betook himself to the orchard, and

lounged back under the apple-trees with his pipe and
some books. Here, half an hour later, Rollo found
him.

"May I come too?" he inquired, knowing that his
presence was not always welcome. "I only want a think
out."

"I should like to cut your brains clean out of your
head for the time you are with me," said Lionel lazily,
as he looked at the earnest eyes and white cheeks of his
nephew. "It would give your body a chance then, and
I should take you back to London a reformed character."

Rollo looked rather downcast. "I don't think I'm
working my brains. I don't feel them. I won't talk."

A silence fell on the pair. Rollo squatted down at a
respectful distance from his uncle ; presently, he lay full
length on the ground chest downwards, and a little later
rolled over on his back and stared up into the sky. He
seemed ill at ease, and his uncle, who was covertly
watching him, at last thought fit to speak.

"Well," he said, "you had better relieve your mind,
so out with it."

Rollo sat up eagerly. "You won't mind if I talk a
little?"

"Fire ahead?"

"It's—it's about 'living together.' The sermon, you
know—and can't boys listen to sermons without being
prigs? Bobby says they can't."

"I think it is not the listening that makes them prigs.
Perhaps the descanting on them afterwards to their
schoolfellows would be priggish!"

"I don't see it," said Rollo perplexedly. "Shall I be
a prig if I speak to you about it?"

"Not necessarily."

"Well, look here, how can we live together with Jesus Christ if He is in heaven, and we are on earth? and what has His dying to do with it? The clergyman said He died to bring us into 'close touch'—those were his words—'close touch' with Himself. I should think 'close touch' means near enough to touch Him, doesn't it?"

"That's about it. Perhaps the other way about would be correct. Near enough to let Him touch us."

"But how can we be as near as that?"

"Do you ever pray, Rollo?"

"Yes, I say my prayers at my bed, you know, but I sometimes pray at other times."

Rollo lowered his voice, and the blood mounted to his cheeks. He added shyly, "I prayed as I walked the other night just before I met the doctor, when I thought you were lost, and God answered me pretty quick."

"How could He hear you if He was so far away?"

Rollo's eyes brightened.

"Oh, well, of course He is always close to us; close enough to speak to."

"Then why not close enough to touch?"

"Really touch?"

"Yes, really touch your soul. That's the part that must live together with Him, not so much your body, though your soul ought to rule that. How are you tempted? Your wrongdoing generally comes from inside, and your soul is too weak to resist temptation. A touch from Christ will make it strong."

"I should like to have a strong soul," said Rollo earnestly.

There was silence again, then Rollo remarked, "Jesus died for us; He was punished for our sins, that's what Miss Percy always says; to let us go to heaven, she says, but the clergyman seemed to say different."

"Not at all," said Lionel, rousing himself, and forgetting in his interest that he was only talking to a small boy with too much brain. "That's the mistake half of us make. Some think His death began and ended with the punishment of our sins, and the belief in that is the only necessity in our lives. . That is the foundation truth, the starting-point, but what we were hearing about this morning was much more than that. Christ did not come down from heaven to live and to die for us, and then go back to His throne and leave us to get on here by ourselves as well as we could. He died that He might purchase us for Himself, we are told. He wants us to live our lives down here, and He helps us from the cradle to the grave, our unseen friend it is true, but a very real one for all that. I've been thinking it out for myself this morning. ' Lo I am with you alway,' He told His disciples, ' even unto the end of the world.' He lives together with us, and we with Him. And from the time we trust Him with our sins, He wants nothing to separate us from His companionship. This is what makes, or ought to make, holy lives."

How much of this Rollo took in was difficult to say. But he startled his uncle in a few minutes by saying, ' Then Jesus Christ is walking through Devonshire with you and me?"

"Let us believe it, and act upon it without over much talk," said his uncle, relapsing into silence, and Rollo subsided.

CHAPTER VIII

A Happy
Old Woman

EARLY Monday morning, Rollo and his uncle were off on their travels. Bobby walked through the village with them. As they passed the " Black Bull " both the landlord and his wife were at the door. Rollo looked across at them, then brought his pony to a standstill.

"Uncle, have you one of your messages I could take that woman? She was rather nasty to me, but the doctor said she had been turned sour by her little girl dying."

Lionel put his hand in his pocket, and gave the boy a little book. He trotted across the road well satisfied.

"Good morning, please. My uncle turned up all right, and we're going away."

"Ay, so ye be, sir, an' me wife be sorry for her quick words. I wish 'ee well, sir."

"'Tis best to be on the safe side," said Mrs. Bentley, looking at Rollo dejectedly, "but if I'd a-known as ye knowed the doctor——"

"It doesn't matter," said Rollo cheerfully, "I just came over to wish you goodbye, and to leave you a message from my uncle. At least, he carries them about with him, but I believe they really come from God!"

He put the little book in her hand, and ran away. Husband and wife eyed it with interest. The title brought tears to Mary Bentley's eyes.

"As one whom his mother comforteth, so will I comfort you." She turned into the house, took it up to her bedroom, and when her day's work was done went upstairs and read it.

"Well," said Bobby, as a crossways was reached, the signal for his dismissal. "I think it's a stunning shame you don't take me with you! I could take Rollo off your hands a bit, Mr. Derrick, and I bet I'd make him a little livelier. I wouldn't give him much time for thinking. And as to books, trust me for keeping them away from him. Oh! why can't I be told to have a rest from lesson books? It's awful rot having your own father the doctor."

"Goodbye, Bobby. I do hope we shall come back this way. It's dreadful knowing people and then leaving them. I wish you'd come up to our school in London. I'm sure you'd like it."

Bobby's laugh rang out so merrily that even Lionel joined in it.

"Fancy any chap liking a stuffy schoolroom! Look at what it's done for you! I've twice the flesh and muscle, and you're older than me."

"Ah, well," said Lionel, pitying his nephew's crest-fallen looks, "men don't rise to be great men through their flesh and muscle; it's generally through their knowledge and wits."

Bobby raced off with a parting shout, and Rollo felt in low spirits.

"I think," he suggested meekly, "it would be nice to stay still in the country for a little."

Lionel shook his head.

"We want to see Nature in all her moods and phases; we didn't come down here to live amongst people. We may like a word with them in passing, but you'll have to put up with me as a companion, and no one else, and you knew what to expect when you started with me."

"Oh, it's all right," Rollo said hurriedly. "I really think I like you best. Bobby does pull one about so. I've had five wrestles with him, and lots of small fights; and I've quite twenty bumps and bruises from him, I'm sure. He jumps on you when you don't expect him. Now I don't have that from you."

"No," said Lionel slowly, "I do my jumps in another way."

It was a very hot day. The lanes through which they passed seemed close and stuffy; flies annoyed them, heat simmered slowly upwards, and when they found a halting-place for lunch under a shady tree just inside a field, Rollo flung himself down on the grass with a tired sigh.

"Dandy jogs so, I feel quite achy."

"You'll feel better after lunch," said Lionel con-solingly.

"I should like a glass of milk."

"When you're rested you can run across the field to that small cottage. Do you see a chimney behind those elms? Perhaps they will give you some milk."

Rollo looked and nodded.

F

Lunch over, Lionel stretched himself out for a smoke and a nap. Dandy, tethered to the gate, was munching the long grass and bracken in the hedge. Rollo, pulling his straw hat well over his eyes, marched across the field with a cheery whistle. He found the cottage, but outside it looked deserted. Some fowls were scraping up a flower border. A black cat sat on the top of an old shed and watched his approach with suspicious eyes. Windows and doors were fast shut, and no smoke appeared from the chimney. The boy knocked at the door, and then as no one answered, tried to open it. The latch lifted easily, and he walked in, finding himself in a tidy little kitchen. There was no sound or sight of any one until he fancied he heard a groan from an adjoining room. Very timidly he stepped into it, and there saw lying on the floor an old woman. Pity conquered fear, and he ran forward.

"Have you tumbled down? Can I help you up again?"

The old woman turned her head.

"The Lord be praised!" she ejaculated in a very weak voice. "He has sent His angel at last. And I were that faithless because he didn't come of a sudden."

"I'm not an angel," said Rollo, stooping over her. "I wish I was, and then I could lift you up easy; but I'll try the best I can."

"'Tis me rheumatiz. 'Tis in the joints like, an' won't let they work."

She gave a groan as he tried in vain to raise her.

"No, little master, 'ee be too frail; but 'ee can fetch help, only do 'ee give I that drap o' tea. I were puttin' of 'un to me lips when I went scatter, an' the cup be smashed, an' 'twere my grandmother's; but there be a drap in the pot still. 'Tis tea I be thirstin' bravely for, an' the longin' gotted betwixt me soul an' the texes I were repeatin' along of, an' I were nigh crazed. For 'twas to Happy Land above I thought meself departin' to, an' yet 'twas the tea that I wanted of most."

Rollo's quick eyes soon spied a little brown teapot on the hob. The fire was nearly out, but he poured the lukewarm beverage in another cup, and knelt down holding it to her lips. She drank it greedily, and gave a satisfied sigh when she had drained the last drop.

" Do 'ee fetch some 'un to help me to me legs agen. I be stiff as the poker for sure, an' I've setted on this cruel cold floor for nigh half the day."

" I'll fetch my uncle." And away up the field Rollo tore, not heeding the sun or the flies.

"Come, quick ! quick ! There's an old woman tumbled down and she can't get up again, and she's too big for me to lift."

Lionel stretched himself and yawned. Then he rose to his feet, and once aware of the necessity for speed, his long legs took him very quickly to the cottage. Very tenderly and carefully he lifted the old woman up and got her in a wooden chair. She seemed quite cheerful, and beyond a groan or two from her rheumatic twinges, was evidently very little the worse for her tumble. She never ceased talking from the time she first caught sight of Lionel.

" You're a doctor, I reckon. For sure 'ee have gotted a doctor's way of handlin'. I do have a brave likin' for the doctors. They be gen'lemans, an' pass the time o' day so cheery like. Passon first, doctor second; there be no folk like 'em for us poor critturs. You bain't a doctor? Eh, bless my soul, what be 'ee? A squire?"

"No, not a squire."

"He's a tramp," broke in Rollo; "and so am I, and I came to ask you to give me a glass of milk. At least——"

Rollo looked round the bare little kitchen and hastily added: "Water would do quite as well. I'm so dreadfully thirsty!"

"Bless my soul! Go out in the yard, dearie. There be the pump handy. Milk be scarce in these parts. The misses at the farm yonner do give I a drop o' scald, but I be fair doubled up wi' rheumatics, an' 'tis a brave long walk for I. Her be rather stiff, but 'ee be a praper hearty little gen'leman, an' will be quicker nor I, for sure!"

The "her" was the pump, and Rollo disappeared at once. The old woman went on talking, and Lionel felt such a pity for her weak lonely state, that he set to work, lighted her fire, put a fresh kettle of water on, and tidied up generally before he left her.

She assured him she would do finely now. She lived quite alone, but every evening a nephew working on a farm near called in to see if she wanted anything.

"Eighty-four las' Christmas week, sir! Thank the Lord for keepin' of me. An' hale and hearty but for the rheumatiz. You'm right welcome to come in, if so be 'ee come by agen, sir. I be fair dazed wi' me upset, but folks reckon I be wunnerful spry for me years! An' the Lord do stan' by me remarkable. 'Twas a miracle the little master come in; 'twas the Lord that dooed it. He just bratted of 'un by when I were in need of he!"

Rollo stared at her gravely.

"Do you have Jesus Christ living with you always? We do; He goes about with us. Of course He brought me to you. It wasn't a miracle; He knew you wanted help."

"Bless me soul, 'ee do talk like Passon! But 'tis Gospel fac'. Back along new year time, 'Liza, me third daughter married to John Carter, one o' they Carters o' Hillsboro', an' uppermost stock they be—her come in, an' sez her to me, 'Mother,' her sez, ''tis too lone-like for 'ee here; 'ee must come an' bide long o' me.' 'No,' sez I, ''tisn't lone I be. Me fowls an' me cat be good company as things o' earth goeth. An' the Lord o' Heaven Hisself won't let an old body feel lonesome, when He bideth long o' me!'"

Lionel gripped her by the hand.

"You're a happy old woman," he said. "Many a crowned head would like to lie on your pillow. Good-day, and thank you for a bit of cheer by the way."

He put something in her hand, then called Rollo, and both took their departure.

"What did you give her?" asked Rollo as they crossed the fields together. "Another message?"

"No; she did not need one. I think she is more in want of food for her poor old body than for her soul, so I gave her that."

"And a message from God is soul food," said Rollo thoughtfully. "People don't always want those kind of messages then?"

"It was my turn for a message," Lionel said; "she gave one to me."

Rollo's face brightened.

"I think it's nicer to get messages than to give them ; I didn't know messengers got messages. Postmen never get letters, do they ? "

"Well, now use your brains a little," said Lionel, with a short laugh. "Do milkmen drink milk, bakers eat bread, shoemakers wear their shoes out——"

Rollo interrupted, "But doctors and clergymen don't want medicine and sermons."

"You ask the next one you come across what he thinks about it. When messengers think themselves above receiving messages, there is something very wrong with them. Don't you go through life thinking it is your *rôle* to do good to others, and that you need nothing yourself from them. We all can learn more than we can teach, to the end of the chapter."

Rollo struggled to understand this, but Lionel's last word brought a sparkle to his eyes.

"Tell you what!" he said ; "our book must have a chapter on messengers."

"Yes ; we must put them in."

"And whenever we meet people on the road," said Rollo eagerly, "we ought either to give them a message or get one from them."

"That's about it," was his uncle's brief reply as, having reached their halting-place, he untied Dandy's halter and made preparations for another start.

That afternoon was a tiring one to both. Their way led along a straight high-road ; the trees were few and far between, and the sun shone down upon them with uncomfortable fierceness. At last Rollo said in a weak little voice, "Dandy is jogging me so. May I get down and walk ? I'm a bit headachy."

Lionel looked at his white face with compunction.

" I'm afraid we're a good four miles from the village I want to get to. If we pass a farmhouse we could stop and have a cup of tea. Cheer up, the sun will soon be going down, and then it will be cooler."

Presently a dark belt of fir-trees came in view; a thick plantation of them bordered one side of the road. As they came up to them the dusky shade and coolness through their aromatic stems made Lionel pause and consider. He was a man of prompt action. In five minutes he had placed Rollo comfortably at the foot of one of them, and Dandy was tethered close by.

" You shall have a good rest before we go on. We will both take a midday nap, and wake up refreshed and cool."

Rollo curled himself up with a weary sigh, rested his head on his uncle's knee, and was in another five minutes fast asleep.

Lionel sat meditating and smoking. He pulled a little book from his pocket. The stillness and hush under the tall slender pines quieted and rested his spirit ; the words from his small book fed it.

A little later he too slept.

The sun began to sink, sending his shafts of light, like golden arrows through the brown firs ; rabbits peeped out of their holes and darted from one hiding-place to another, and then along a little well-worn track stepped a young girl. She was reading as she walked, so her progress was necessarily slow.

Suddenly she raised her head, and confronted the two sleepers. She started violently, and the light of recognition sparkled in her eye.

CHAPTER IX

Lionel's
Golden Gorse

A S she stood there in her white dress and hat, with her sunny brown hair clustering round her little ears and neck, she looked, with her startled brown eyes, like some shy wood nymph. The pink colour ebbed and flowed in her fair face as she gazed at the sleepers. Her lips quivered, she glanced around her anxiously, then looked again, not at the child, but at the man, with deep emotion.

Under the spell of those earnest eyes, what man could sleep?

Lionel opened his eyes, and for the moment thought he was dreaming.

" Effie ! " he exclaimed, rising to his feet, and striding towards her. " Tell me it is not your ghost ! Is it really you in flesh and blood ? "

" Do I look like a ghost ? " was the bright reply ; and for an instant she turned away her blushing cheeks.

" But—but I left you in London ? "

" Yes, and I thought you were in town still. Uncle had a slight attack of influenza, and came down here to get rid of it. We are staying with a cousin of his, a clergyman, and the Rectory is only half an hour's walk from here."

" Is it at Dudley Barton?   That is our next stopping-place."

" Yes—oh, why did you not come sooner?   We go on to Farntower to-morrow."

" Let us be thankful we have met at all," said Lionel gladly, and then he came closer to the girl.

" Are you pleased to see me, Effie ? "

" Is not any one pleased to see the face of a friend in a strange country ? "

As he stepped nearer her, she stepped back.   There was a mixture of fun and seriousness in her tone.

But Lionel would not be trifled with.   Here under the pines his golden gorse was blossoming.   What would a few pricks signify, if he could at last come to close quarters ?

" For the past two years our meetings have invariably been in a crowd.   Now here alone, Effie, I ask you to deal truly and sweetly with me.   Your uncle is not present.   Be your free natural self for once.   Give me a word of hope."

She was standing now with her hands clasped behind her against a pine.   Her book had fallen to the ground, and her wonderful tell-tale eyes for one instant met his in a swift upward glance.

Yet something in her slight, upright figure, an undefinable "touch-me-not" attitude, kept him just two feet away from her.

" I cannot bid you hope," she said in a quick crisp tone.   " I am tied and bound as you know to a tyrannical yet loving old relative, who will not suffer any other man across his threshold.   I am his nurse, his companion, his slave ; he holds me to my promise made five years ago when he was so ill, that I would not leave him till he died. He has forbidden you the house, and he has forbidden me to go to Mrs. Vaughan's because he discovered that I met you there. What hope can I give you?"

"You can assure me that you think of me often—always; that you will wait as I will wait, till he changes his mind, or till he requires your services no longer."

"Till he dies? Oh, Lionel, do not wish for his death."

"Honestly in the sight of God I do not. Poor, miserable jealous old man, perhaps this bit of his life is the happiest he has ever experienced. It would be so, I know to me, could I but change places with him."

A tender wistful smile was in his eyes and on his lips at the thought. For a moment there was silence, then he took a step forward, and lightly brought the girl's hands from behind her back, and held them in his own.

"Now, dear one, here we are, pulse to pulse, with no one to thrust us from each other, and God's own blessing waiting to fall upon us. Dare you say under these pines, in this silent wood that we have not been brought together for a purpose this afternoon? We love each other. I have told you of my love before, though you have tried to frustrate every attempt I have made in that direction. You love me. Your sweet honest eyes have told me so. I have learnt to see your very soul through them, and you cannot deceive me. Now give yourself to me as if we stood at God's altar. Circumstances may still divide our bodies, but our souls and spirits will be linked together. We can afford to wait if we are secure in each other's love and faithfulness."

His tone vibrated with passion and fervour.

A quiver passed through her frame. She resisted no longer. He felt as he pressed her trembling hands in his that the tension relaxed, and she was conquered.

"Why will you make me put into words what you ought to have known long ago?" she said, making a feeble effort to smile.

"I want the words," he said briefly, with great self-control.

"I would not have let you take my hands in such a masterful grip, if—if my heart had not been ready to accompany them."

He smiled then, and stooped his face.

Lips met, and a dual existence for each commenced from that moment never in their case to terminate throughout eternity.

When Rollo awoke he was astonished to hear the murmur of voices. But for the moment he could see no one, so he scrambled to his feet and prepared to reconnoitre.

Behind some pines he saw his uncle in eager converse with a stranger. He stepped forward, and was surprised at the start he gave them. Was it possible that there was just a little frown on his uncle's forehead as he caught sight of his nephew?

"Run away, Rollo. I am talking to a friend."

"*I* must run away, Lionel, don't keep me, and let me speak to this small nephew."

She held out her hand to Rollo, but he turned his back on her, and ran as if for his life.

Lionel smiled.

"He is an intensely obedient child, is he not? Why should you go so soon?"

"I must. I came out for a walk with a book. I shall barely get back in time for tea, and uncle always likes me to read to him afterwards. It was the shade and coolness of these pines that tempted me. How little I thought they would contain *you!*"

"We will come a part of the way with you."

Hastily Lionel went back to Rollo and Dandy.

"Come along as quickly as you can. I have met a friend. Ride on in front of us. You can't mistake the way, it is a straight road."

Rollo mounted his pony and obeyed his uncle without a word.

The road was cooler now, a soft breeze had sprung up, and the sun began to lose its power.

"It is getting sleepy," said Rollo to himself as he watched it sinking slowly behind the belt of pines.

He did not look behind him, but when a certain lane was reached, he heard the two behind him come to a standstill, and wish each other goodbye.

"How far from here is Farntower?"

"An hour's journey by train. It is no good, Lionel. You must not attempt to follow us."

"It is preposterous that you and I should be wandering about Devonshire almost within earshot, and not be together. I shall not make any promises to keep away from Farntower. Where do you stay?"

"At the 'Red Dragon,' it is a delicious old country inn, they say. Uncle has been there before. We have the most lovely view of the moor."

The voices dropped to a lower key. Rollo rode steadily on. Presently as he came in sight of a village, his uncle overtook him.

"Now we will put up at the inn and have a substantial tea.   How is your head?   Better?"

"Quite well, thank you."

Lionel was in the best of spirits, but Rollo was very quiet.   They entered the inn, which was in the village street, and were shown into a private parlour looking out into an old-fashioned garden behind, full of holly-hocks and sunflowers.

Rollo curled himself up on a low broad window-seat, and put his head out of the open window.

Lionel ordered a meal, then restlessly paced the garden walks.   Rollo looked at him in thoughtful wonder.

When they were busily refreshing themselves with a dish of eggs and bacon, tea and bread-and-butter, Rollo's tongue was loosed.

"Did you give her a message, or did she give you one, uncle?"

"We both gave each other one," said Lionel, looking across at his nephew curiously.

"She looked like a fairy," went on Rollo.   "I suppose you really did know her before."

"Why do you question it?"

"Because she came to meet you in the wood. Witches do that, and fairies; they turn themselves into beautiful ladies; they always do it in woods. I was afraid perhaps——"

"Oh, you need not be afraid.   Queens and lovely princesses wander about in woods, and sometimes meet the one they are looking for."

"And then?" questioned Rollo eagerly.

"I will leave you to finish the tale."

Something in his uncle's tone silenced the boy. When tea was over he ran out into the garden, and there, on a wooden seat close to some beehives, sat an old crippled man. Rollo marched up and shook hands with him.

"How do you do? We are tramps, my uncle and I. And we're going to sleep here to-night. Are you sleeping here too?"

"'Tis eighty year come Michaelmas that I've a-slep' an' eat an' drunk in yonner house."

He nodded solemnly after giving this information.

Rollo looked at him and pondered. "Does it belong to you? Have you never been away from it?"

"Belang to I!"

The old man rose in fury. He beat his stick against the bench to add emphasis to his words.

"Do this 'ere 'Red Rose' belang to I? Ask that old dawg lyin' there, they dratted fowl, that be so busy scratchin' up the beans, they'll tell 'ee there be not a blessed piece o' chiny or furnitur in that there house that didn't belang to I 'fore Johnnie and his missus were borned! Belang to I! In course it do. I bratted me missus when her were a little maid wi' pink cheek an' curly hair to the 'Red Rose,' when Joe Simmett were a-layin' down his brush from paintin' of 'un. I mind the smell o' the fresh paint now. Sez I to she, 'Smell me Rose, Sue?' An' her giveth a sniff—'Ay, that I do, tu!' sez her. An' I took her roun' the neck an' giv' un a smacking kiss. 'But this be the purtiest rose to 'me,' sez I. Ay, an' I mind——"

The old man sat down again and became slightly incoherent in his recollections.

Rollo took a seat by his side. "I like people when

they're very old," he said confidentially, as he swung his legs to and fro, "because they know such a lot. And I like to hear what the world was like before I came into it—what was this house like eighty years ago?"

The old man responded eagerly, in no ways taken aback.

"The coaches did come by, I mind, an' brave an' gay they made the road wi' they horns a-buglin', an' the horses steamin' an' sweatin', an' the drivers a-swearin' an drinkin', an' crackin' their jokes wi' I! Ay, them were the days fur I! The ladies an' the gents from Lunnon, an' oftentimes a suspecty characky wi' his cloak up to eyes of 'un, an' a voice in the boots of 'un! An' I mind Great George—ever heard tell of 'un, little master? Saint George he called hisself, but he were the tither way round most folks did reckon; there warn't much saint of he! He rode a black hoss, an' he did paint 'un white, an' red, an' yaller by turn, to make fools of us. Ess, fay! He were a bold 'un! Many a time did I give 'un a drink, an' nex' news were the coach overturned, an' the passengers an' they vallybles so mixed, that when they sorted theyselves an' gotted to they legs, an' helped by a perlite stranger, why, what follers? The passengers left, an' the vallybles taken, an' never did they sot eyes on they money an' joolry an' such like agen! An' nex' day Great George come ridin' up.

"'Heard the noos?' sez 'un to I. 'Terrible state o' things in a Christian country!' sez 'un; 'these scoundrels must be ketched and hung!' he sez, an' then he rideth off wi' that big laugh o' his'n. Ay, dearie me, back along those days were real good 'uns!"

" I love hearing about it," said Rollo enthusiastically.
" How I wish there were robbers and highwaymen about
now! Fancy, if uncle and I were to meet one on a dark
night! I wish we could! What was Great George like!"

" He were nigh on seven foot, an' his hoss were to
match. He had a big laugh, an' a soft voice like a
woman's, an' nobody couldn't catch of 'un!"

" An' what became of him!"

" I never heerd tell. Some did say he were thrown in
a bog, some that he turned Methody an' giv' up his sins,
an' some that his horse were shot, an' he couldn't make
up his mind to ride another!"

" I suppose it was wicked of him," said Rollo thoughtfully. " But I do like hearing about it. I wish there
could be good robbers. They're so much more exciting
than any one else. I would like to be one myself!"

The old man was back in the doleful present again.

" Folks be different now, 'tis Johnnie this, an'
Johnnie that, an' young Tom, me eldest gran'son, be
more count than I! Tom be goin' to marry nex' week,
an' his sweetheart never so much as passed the time o'
day wi' I. But her took count of I, an' sez she to
Tom—

" ' Your gran'feyther be a burden to ye all,' sez she
—the young hussy! Sez I the nex' time I catcheth
sight on her—

" ' Not so big a burden as them idle rattypates that
eats their husban's vittles, an' empties his purse over
ribbons an' flowers, an' maketh fun o' the man that
putted together the money for they to squander!'"

Down came the stick with such vehemence that Rollo
started to his feet.

"'Tis said," continued the old man, who always quoted Scripture when his wrongs proved too much for his feelings, "'the last shall be first, and the first last,' an' the old man that be put aside an' shoved in corners, will be righted up yonner, an' will trample his enemies underfoot!"

"I expect you'll get there first, before any of us," Rollo said, eyeing him respectfully.

This did not seem to comfort the old man. He shook his head.

"They be all wantin' me in the grave," he said in quavering tones. "'Tis cruel hard on I!"

"But you'll be in heaven, not in the grave," said Rollo brightly. "I should ask God to take you very soon, 'specially if you aren't happy. I wouldn't mind going to heaven to-morrow. Miss Percy told me when I was ill—and I used to get rather frightened, because I heard the doctor say he couldn't pull me through—she told me that you go fast asleep and wake up in heaven."

"Aye, but it be an awesome place to find meself in, wi' Bible folks an' such like, an' I never could bide strangers!"

"But Jesus will be there," the boy said eagerly and softly. "You know Him."

"I bain't a scholar, an' I bain't acquainted wi' Him."

There was a little wistfulness in the old man's tone. He added—

"Heaven be a brave long way off from I!"

"But," pursued Rollo, "Jesus is here now close to us. He walks along every day with us, wherever we are. We don't talk about it, uncle and I; we said it was best not to, but when we're quiet we think about it a lot. If

G

you just think He is close to you, it makes it very nice. You can't help knowing Him, and it makes you want to be awfully good ! "

The old man shook his head in hopeless despair.

" 'Tis too hard.   I bain't a scholar."

" Oh well, I can't say it any different.   I know He's here close to you, and you can't make Him a long way off anyhow, so if you want to speak to Him you can."

Rollo was called indoors by his uncle ; he nodded to the old man, and ran off.

It was bedtime, and soon in a big bed in an old-fashioned room, Rollo slept deeply and well.

CHAPTER X

Kizzy the Nurse

" IT looks as if we are in for a spell of good weather."
" Yes, wouldn't it be nice to live quite out of
doors? Tell you what! We could camp out like
gypsies."

Lionel did not rise to this bait.

" Do you think you could get on without me for a day
or two, Rollo?"

" I s'pose I could. Should Dandy and I tramp on
without you?"

" No, I should make arrangements for you to stay at
a farm or inn. I don't think I would leave you here.
I want to go about eight miles further to-day. An old
nurse of mine lives about that distance off, and I
thought she would take care of you for a day or two."

" I don't want to be nursed," said Rollo, with injured
dignity. " I would get on by myself very well indeed.
Are you going away?"

" Only by train somewhere; I may be away a couple
of days."

Rollo looked curiously at his uncle. They were at
breakfast the next morning; Lionel seemed absent-
minded. He poured out a cup of hot water and passed
it to his little nephew instead of tea; he had tried to

read a newspaper upside down, and had not responded to any of the boy's remarks. Rollo shook his head in quaint fashion.

"I'm afraid he's tired of me," was his thought; but he said nothing.

They left the inn directly after breakfast. Rollo went out to wish his old friend goodbye. He was feebly walking up and down the gravel paths talking to himself as he did so.

Rollo handed him a little book.

"I asked my uncle to give it to me for you. It's a message. My uncle is a kind of messenger besides being a tramp. He carries messages in his pockets for people. You'll see what it's about. I don't quite know myself, but I know who it comes from."

"Eh? Thank'ee, little master. It do come from yer uncle I reckon. Thank 'un kindly."

"No," said Rollo, "he's brought it to you, but it really comes from God."

He ran away. The old man opened the little paper book with trembling fingers. He read—

"Let not your heart be troubled: ye believe in God, believe also in Me. In My Father's house are many mansions: if it were not so, I would have told you. I go to prepare a place for you."

"To think on't," he mused. "There be some 'un ready wi' a home for I. They be wantin' to be rid o' I down here, that be truth. Ay, I mindeth these words. My mother did tell I to read 'em back along when her were took for death. I doth believe in God, so I doth! The little lad spoke about the Lord bein' brave an' near to I. 'Twouldn't be no harm puttin' up a kind o' prayer to 'un to ax for my place to be kep' for I. 'Tis a kindly comfortin' thought not to let me heart be troubled 'bout sich matters. So, great Lord, I herewise humbly speak to 'Ee, an' ax 'Ee kindly to mind that there 'ouse for I. I be not particklar as to a mansion. 'Tis too big for I. An' a small 'un be more home like. An' I ax 'Ee humbly not to make too much ado in preparin', for I do be a poor old wicked sinner, an' I doth not expec' overmuch, an' I'd be humbly obliged if 'Ee would teach me to pray praper. For Christ's sake. Umun."

Rollo and his uncle were pursuing their way along a true Devonshire lane. The uninteresting high-road was left; on either side of them rose banks of luxuriant green. Ferns of all sorts hung above them, delicate-veined ivy rioted amongst the moss, and wild roses and honeysuckle peeped out at intervals. The lane wound up and down in the true Devonshire way. Lionel was silent and abstracted. Rollo was busy wondering what the nurse was like, whether she would curtail his freedom and treat him like a baby, or recognise that he was of an age to be independent of women. At last he gave a heavy sigh.

"I thought I had done with women for a time," he said; "but we're always meeting them."

Lionel roused himself at once.

"What do you mean by that?" he demanded sharply. "Is it anything to you whom I meet or speak to?"

"I was only thinking of this nurse," answered Rollo meekly. "I hope I shan't find her a cross person."

Lionel's brow cleared. He had forgotten the existence of the nurse; to him at present there was only one woman in the universe.

"I must find out where she lives," he said. "Her name will be a help. I should not think there could be many Keziah Kingcups."

Rollo pondered over the name. It did not recommend her to his favour. He was not sorry when that morning ride was over. They came to a cosy little village with a cluster of thatched cottages crowding round an old grey church, whilst on the distant hills were substantial-looking farmhouses. Lionel went into a little general shop to make inquiries. He came out with a bright face.

"She is here," he said; "lives about half a mile out of the village. Come along; I have no time to waste, as the station is nearly two miles off and I want to catch the afternoon train."

Off they went, through the village, up another lane, across a bridge, and finally stopped at a picturesque old cottage nearly smothered in trees and creepers. Lionel went up a little cobble path and tapped at a half-open door. A tall old woman appeared, and gazed at him with dim inquiring eyes.

"Well, Kizzy, don't you know me?"

A light came into her face, and she grasped his hand.

"Mr. Lionel! As sure as life! Come 'ee in, sir, an' sit 'ee down. Eh dear, what a day! 'Scuse me tremblin' a bit, sir. Surprises be rayther sudden, an' I be not so young as I were!"

"I want to know if you can put up my small nephew for a day or two, Kizzy. You remember his mother, Miss Sybil?"

"Eh, dearie me, what a day! A boy o' Miss Sybil's, an' I seem to see her now a-rushin' up to me as I were a-puttin' a stitch to her weddin' gown. 'Kizzy!' her says, a-throwin' her arms roun' me neck, 'shall I give him up an' stay at home? I really can't leave you all,' her says in her pretty earnest way. An' is this the little gentleman? Come in, sir, an' I would take shame on myself if I couldn't give a bit o' me roof to Miss Sybil's son!"

Dandy was led round to the back of the house, and Rollo found himself in a cheery-looking kitchen with a smouldering wood fire, and everything immaculately clean and shining. Lionel explained very hurriedly that he wished to leave his little nephew for a couple of days in Keziah's care, and she willingly agreed.

"You are sure to come back?" Rollo questioned doubtfully, as Lionel wished him goodbye.

His uncle laughed.

"Humanly speaking, I am certain to do so. Don't give any trouble, and ride out with Dandy each day to give him exercise.

He was gone. Rollo sat on a wooden chair, feeling rather forlorn.

"Cheer up," said Keziah, standing opposite him, with folded arms and critical eye. "That be my maxim handed down from me gran'mother. You do be a little like your mother, sir. Now, will 'ee bide here while I get a room upstair ready, an' then us must have some dinner. An' it be remarkable that I've a hot little egg and bacon pasty in the oven, which your dear mother did used to delight in."

Rollo was hungry, and the egg and bacon pasty sounded delightful.

"It isn't so bad," he announced to himself, when she had disappeared. "She isn't quite a stranger. I dare-

say mother was quite happy to be with her when she
was a little girl, so I ought to be."

Keziah did not leave him long alone. She soon had
a clean cloth spread on the deal table, and besides the
pasty produced a plain currant cake, some cheese, and
some ripe gooseberries. Rollo enjoyed his dinner; and
his tongue being loosed, he was soon on the most
confidential terms with this tall old woman, who chatted
on so incessantly.

Dinner over, he went out into the yard to look after
Dandy; then pushing open a tiny gate he found himself
in an orchard. Apples hung on every tree, and bees
and butterflies caroused in an old-fashioned flower
border that ran along the side of the orchard.

Here, half an hour later, Keziah, with some knitting
under her arm, found him lying full length on the grass.

"Us will have a bit o' talk again," she said cheerily,
pulling out an old wooden stool from a bed of nettles,
and planting herself upon it with great care and delibera-
tion. "I be fond o' this spot, for it be shady most
times, and the sun be wonderful warm to-day."

"Yes," said Rollo; "I think I'd rather be here than
riding along dusty roads. I wonder why Uncle didn't
take me with him?"

" 'Tis difficult to see into young men's minds,"
asserted Keziah. "Mr. Lionel were always a strong-
willed boy, and able to manage his own affairs, from the
day he told me he could part his hair straighter than
what I did."

"I'm a little afraid he may be tired of me," said
Rollo, sitting up with his back against an apple-tree, and
prepared to hold forth. "You see, he met a friend

yesterday in a wood, and he has been a little bit—well, not exactly cross, but not quite such friends with me since."

"Who was the friend?" asked Keziah, with interest.

"She was all in white; she looked very pretty."

Keziah's eyes twinkled. She nodded her head up and down with great vigour.

"I knewed it. There was that in his voice, in his eyes, in the way he tooked no notice o' nothin', an' in the tearin' haste he departed—it all told me of his state. I've seen too many that have bin tooked that way!"

"What way? Do you think he is ill?"

Rollo's eyes were big with wonder.

"Bless 'ee, no; not ill as 'ee mean, but he be took with the young man's epidemic. It do come sure as life to they all!"

"What is it?" asked Rollo, in no way comforted.

"He be *in love*," was the solemn, emphatic reply.

"I'm afraid I don't understand."

"No, an' 'tis a long way off from 'ee, sir, for which give thanks. 'Tis a terrible wearin' thing. If so be as it go too smooth, 'tis bad for the parties concerned, they be sure to come to differences later, an' if 'tis rough, an' hedged up like, 'tis tryin' to the temper an' habits. But there be nothin' to do an' say, but just look on, an' advise 'em well, an' be patient. 'Tis no use whatsomever to choke or stop it. Might as well try to push a express train back with your ten fingers, or stop a river's flow with a stone!"

"But what is it?" questioned Rollo a little impatiently.

"Well, 'tis what folks feel for each other afore they

be married. 'Tisn't often it lasts a long ways afterwards. Not as a rule, I'm thinkin'; but I wouldn't speak certainly on that score, bein' a single woman meself, but judgin' much from quick observation."

"Is Uncle Lionel going to be married?"

"Ay, but that be too quick a way to put it, sir."

"To the lady we met yesterday," said Rollo, a light breaking over his face, "and he's gone to see her to-day. Now I understand."

Keziah nodded at him with a smile, and knitted on in silence for a few minutes, then she said—

"'Tis to be hoped her'll be a blessin' to him. Women make a man from his cradle to his grave!"

Rollo looked at her respectfully.

"She was, of course, very nice, but it's a pity Uncle Lionel met her. I liked him best when he had no woman to think of. I don't mean to be rude about women. I like them sometimes, but not when we're just two without them. And Uncle Lionel has been so quiet since yesterday. He wouldn't talk and laugh with me at all. Do you think they're being married now?"

"Bless 'ee, sir, not quite so fast! 'Tis only a-guessin' and presumin' us be! Maybe he may be in love with she, an' she with some 'un else. 'Tis no accountin' for tastes. 'Tis a strange thing, after all said an' done, that some takes such a violent fancy to some, an' others thinks nothin' at all about 'em, but 'ee can't place no dependence on such a thing as love."

"It's a very stupid kind of thing, I should think," said Rollo gravely.

"Well," said Kizzy, who was settling into one of her

moralising moods, "that's as 'ee look at it. It takes
some away from theirselves an' makes 'em think of
others first, an' that be a good thing. To my mind,
'tis good to have another to please, an' to think about.
But, then, if one makes too much o' the other, the
t'other gets selfish an' puffed up sometimes, an' so what
be doin' one on 'em good be doin' the t'other harm."

"I'm afraid I don't quite understand," said Rollo,
with wrinkled eyebrows.

"No, sir, an' 'tisn't to be expec'ed 'ee should. Time
enough yet for little lads like yourself. But those be
some on my thoughts, an' young lovers think there be
no one but them in the whole wide world, an' no one
else don't count at all, not even their fathers an' mothers
an' brothers an' sisters. They can all make 'emselves
scarce, an' they'll be happier for their absence, which is
a evil state o' things!"

"It seems rather a wrong kind of thing," admitted
Rollo; "but Uncle Lionel is a good man, and he won't
do anything that isn't quite right."

"Eh, no sir! Us won't think of such a thing at all,
an' I be the last one to hold back happiness from such
a nice young gentleman as he have grown up to be.
They do say that marriages be made from Heaven, an
if this be from above, then God bless 'em both, I say."

But Rollo could not amen this. He sat with his
knees drawn up and his chin resting on them, and he
looked up at the summer sky as if his thoughts were far
away.

At last he spoke.

"It's a pity she interrupted us. We were tramping
together first-rate. I s'pose he'd rather not have me

any more. I wonder if he'd give me enough money to go on alone. But it would be rather dull."

"Eh, sir? don't 'ee be so downcast! Mr. Lionel won't forsake you. He'll come back as bright as a button, sure as life he will! That is, if her'll have him, an' her won't be worth much if her don't!"

"I s'pose this Love is quite a grown-up thing. It's one of the things with no fun in it," Lionel pursued. His mind was too full of the subject to dismiss it lightly. "There are so many things that grown-up people like doing that seem very strange and dull to me. Like sitting up and talking in their best clothes, and listening to dry lectures and sermons, and sitting up, smoking, and doing, and saying nothing, while they do it."

"But 'tis not a dull thing, by no means," said Keziah, with a little laugh. "It brings light into sad eyes, an' smiles an' pretty looks out o' the plainest face, an' it makes a rough man's voice tender an' soft, an' it waxes eloquent the weak an' timid, an' 'tis a beautiful thing altogether when it's the right sort."

Rollo sighed dejectedly; then his face brightened. "It would make a chapter in our book, if—if Uncle will help me to write it. I will ask him when he comes back."

"There be my best hen a-crowin' over a egg her's laid! I must be off, for she do lay it in such outlandish places, that if I don't get up to her quick, I spend my day in lookin' for it."

Keziah bustled off, and Rollo followed her, shaking off his depression of spirits as he did so, and resolving to put such a weighty and inexplicable matter as "Love" far away from him for the present.

CHAPTER XI

Alf, the Gypsy

" NOW what ought I to do! It's just like the picture of the Good Samaritan hung up in my little room at Kizzy's; only I'm not a man, and Dandy isn't a donkey, and he hasn't been robbed."

Rollo's face was a picture of dismay and perplexity. He was on his pony, and was gazing at the recumbent figure of a lad in the ditch. He had been out for a ride, and was coming back along a lonely road when he spied the prostrate form. At first he thought he was asleep, but a groan brought him to a standstill.

"What's the matter? Are you hurt?" he inquired.

The lad raised his head feebly.

"I be taken bad," he moaned; "cruel bad. I can't get no further. I be twisted all over wi' pains."

"But where's your home?"

"Got none."

"Where are you going?"

There was no reply; the lad dropped his head, and his groans increased.

It was at this juncture that Rollo soliloquised with himself. Finally he got off his pony, and stood over the lad.

He was a gypsy; the black curls that clustered over
his head, the small rings in his ears, and a bright yellow
handkerchief knotted round his throat proclaimed the
fact.

But he was a heavy broad-shouldered fellow, and Rollo
shook his head hopelessly.

"I can't lift you up," he said; "but if you would try
to get up yourself, and mount my pony, I would take
you to the village I come from."

The lad opened his eyes, and Rollo had to repeat his
invitation before he understood it. Then with a great
effort he struggled to his feet, and after some difficulty,
and with many determined and ineffectual efforts on
Rollo's part, he hoisted himself on Dandy's back.

Rollo took hold of the bridle, and marched sturdily
along. His thoughts were anxious ones.

"Where had I better take him? The Bible said an
inn. But they wouldn't take care of him for twopence
at the 'Old Fiddler,' I am sure. And I've only
sixpence in my pocket. Kizzy won't like to have him,
I'm afraid. I expect she'll be angry with me, but it
would have been just like the priest and the Levite to
see him there, and pass him by!"

He at last resolved to go straight to Keziah.

"If she won't take him in, she will tell me what to do
with him," he wisely thought, and this conclusion seemed
the right one.

Keziah met them at the gate with scared face and
uplifted hands, but when she saw the plight of the gypsy
lad her woman's heart was touched.

"He do look bad, as sure as life! But 'tis the
Infirmary he must be took to. An' for all 'ee can tell,

sir, he may be full o' infection an' disease. 'Tis a
misfortune for 'ee to have met with him."

Rollo did not take the same view.

Whilst they were talking, a little man came cantering
down the road on a big black horse. Keziah darted out
after him.

"Doctor! Doctor Parkings! 'Tis Providence have
sent 'ee! Come in, sir, please, an' have a look at this
lad!"

Dr. Parkings stopped; the lad was taken into the
back kitchen, and a consultation was held over him.
The result was highly satisfactory.

He has had a bad fall, but there is nothing fractured.
You need not be alarmed, he isn't sickening for anything."

"'Twas from a haystack," murmured the lad, "but I
walked a mile afore I give in!"

"Well, you will have to give in for a couple of days,
for you have strained some muscles, and they must have
rest. Where are your friends?"

"Gone on the road to Exeter."

"Are you tramping the country?"

"Ay."

"I think you had better be moved to the Infirmary
without delay."

"No thank 'ee, not if I know it. I'll be crawlin' on
as best I can, but to them Government places I don't
go. Never been in gaol yet, an' don't mean to go, nor
yet yer 'firmaries an' sich like!"

He raised his head in excited protest, then sank back
with a groan. Rollo's thoughtful little voice made
itself heard—

" Kizzy, could he have my room, do you think ? Just
for one night or two.   I could sleep on the sofa in your
parlour.   I should like to."

Kizzy looked at the doctor.

" I'm a human bein'," she said ; " an' I tries to foller
the example in the blessed Gospels ; but I never have
taken an unknown tramp in yet, for I be a lone woman,
an' my little home with its vallybles be precious."

" Oh, Kizzy, let him stay," Rollo pleaded, " do let
him stay ; I'll look after him—I'm sure he would like to
stay."

The lad raised his head again.

" I had best be off."

Whether it was his dark eyes and curls—Kizzy said
afterwards that she always had a weakness for black
eyes and hair—or whether it was his helplessness, one or
the other melted her heart.

" My lad, ye'll stay wi me," she said, with decision ;
" but it'll be a poor reward if ye touches one o' my
fowls, an' I have but one silver spoon in the house, an'
that be on the mantelshelf, so now ye know my mind,
and I'll make up a bed in the back kitchen, an' there ye
shall bide, till us sees what two days' rest an' food will do
for 'ee."

The little doctor looked dubious, but Keziah was now
quite certain of her own mind, and he gave her his
parting directions saying he would call in the next day.
Rollo's face was radiant, and when Keziah had made the
lad thoroughly comfortable for the night, Rollo went in
to see him.

" Are you feeling better now ?   Will you tell me your
name ? "

" Alf Castle."

" What a nice name! I thought you would like to know that I'm a kind of tramp like you are. My uncle and I are tramping every day, but he's gone away for two days and left me here. I wonder if I hadn't seen you, who would have come along."

Alf looked brighter and better already. He lay gazing at Rollo with a spark of humour in his eye.

" And where be ye goin' ? " he demanded.

" Nowhere. We just go on every day, and we meet with fresh people, and then we leave them and go on to others. Isn't it a wonder to have such *millions* of people living, and not know about them ? I should never have known you if I hadn't gone down that lane to-day. But I think Jesus made me go there."

" Ye be a rum 'un ! "

" Well, you see it's like this. Jesus Christ is with us. He comes along wherever we go, an' I s'pose He knew you were wanting somebody to find you, so He made me do it."

Alf stared at him in wonder. Rollo's talk drifted on, and soon Alf was feeling well enough to enjoy relating some of his experiences. They were very good friends before Rollo's bedtime came. The next morning a letter arrived from Lionel saying he would not be returning till a day later. And Rollo did not feel this as great a disappointment as he would have done twenty-four hours previously.

Keziah sent him out for a ride in the morning, saying grimly as she watched him down the lane—

" It will be as well to pick up no more strangers, for I couldn't put 'em up ! "

H

Clouds were rolling up for rain, and in the afternoon it came down with a steady, soft persistence. Rollo settled himself down in the back kitchen with great satisfaction.

Alf was already sitting up, and looking with longing eyes through the little window at the green country outside.

"I should die straight away if I lived under a roof like this 'ere!"

"Would you?" asked Rollo, with a look of alarm. "Do you think it's hurting you? Tell me again how you like to live. I love to hear it. It sounds so wild and free."

So Alf dilated on the woods and forests that he loved, the heather-covered moor, and the rugged hills. He spoke of animals and birds that were as yet unknown to the eager boy at his side; of waterfalls and glens, and ruddy fires by night, and as he listened Rollo drew deep breaths of delight.

"I wish—I wish I had been born a gypsy. I can't help thinking sometimes that our tramp is rather quiet and dull. I thought we should meet with so many adventures—robbers, and highwaymen, and wild beasts —but Devonshire seems a very tame place. I should really like to meet with a highwayman on a horse, a real one with a mask and a pistol, just when it's getting dark; or a brigand who would hide us in a cave up a mountain. That would be the best fun. Have you ever seen one? Do you think we might possibly meet with one before I go back to London?"

Alf proceeded to tell with much animation how a Dartmoor convict had come to them for shelter once, and how successfully they had hidden him, until he was able to get shipped off to America. His escapes were hair-breadth ones, and Rollo listened with round eyes and mouth.

"I'm so glad he escaped," he exclaimed. "It must be so dreadful to be hunted as if you were an animal."

"Yer wouldn't give a chap up, would 'ee now, if the coves were arter him wi' handcuffs?"

"No, *never*," said Rollo stoutly.

Alf looked at him curiously, then he lowered his voice.

"See here, young 'un. There may be some fellers arter me—quite a mistake, ye know. Folks is cruel mis-judged. Some on us had a bit o' spite 'gainst a farmer who turned us off a waste bit o' his land that warn't fit fur pigs to grunt on! An' us sarved he right, for two on his ricks were cotched on fire, and there was a hulla-boloo. I were on the top o' one when I got me fall, and t'others made off just afore the farmer came up."

"But what were you doing on the top of the rick?" asked Rollo.

"A-tryin' to put it out, yer stoopid, o'course! An' I crawled through a hedge an' ran for me life until the pain grew worse an' worse, an' down I fell, just like a log. But 'tis ten chances to one if that there farmer don't try to nab me, for he saw me fall, an' likely thought I was up to no good. Folks is that suspicious!"

"But you could easily explain to him that you were trying to put the fire out," said Rollo. "And I don't think he'll know where to find you, so you needn't be afraid."

"If he do come pokin' round, swear that ye won't tell on me!"

"I don't know how to swear," said Rollo naïvely; "I

never learnt.   I don't think I ought to, ought I ?   But
I won't let him in here."

The very next morning Rollo's fidelity to his new
friend was put to the test.   Keziah went out and left
the boys together.   They were talking about stag-
hunting on Exmoor, and Alf was making Rollo's eyes
dilate at the description of a run in which the stag had
got the better of his pursuers, when a sharp knock on
the outer door made them start.

Alf cowered underneath the bedclothes.

" Now young 'un, mind yer oath ! " he whispered.

Rollo ran out into the front kitchen, and with some
trepidation opened the door.

A tall, burly looking-man stood outside.

" Be this Mrs. Keziah Kingcup's ? "

" She is away," said Rollo sturdily.

" A've bin told her hath tooked in a gypsy rascal, an'
'a be come to track 'un out.   He be a praper scoundrel,
an' to gaol he goeth, for three o' me best ricks be
destroyed, an' 'a seed 'un doin' 'un, 'a seed 'un wi his
yaller kerchief, an' 'a hath gotted a bit o' the yaller, torn
by the hedge that he crept through.   'A be goin' to
track 'un sure enough.   Where be 'un ?   Stand aside, little
master.   'A be comin' in."

Then with a flush on his cheek and a light in his eye
Rollo rose to the occasion.   Before the farmer could
know what he was going to do he slammed the door in
his face and locked it.   Then running upstairs to his
little bedroom he put his head out of the window.

" I'm sorry to be rude, Mr. Farmer, but Kizzy is out,
and she wouldn't like strange men coming into her
house.   You must go away.   There's nobody here that

ought to be in gaol. Go away." The farmer shook his fist in anger.

"Don't ye play no tricks on 'a! Ye will be for defyin' the law, wull ye? 'A be goin' straight to the policeman, an' then us shall see if ye be slammin' the door in his face. If Mrs. Kingcup be hidin' a gaolbird, her will be reckoned wi'!"

He strode down the lane with muttered oaths, and Rollo trembled as he looked after him. Then shutting the window he stole down to Alf. He found him struggling into his clothes with feverish haste.

"He has gone off, Alf," said Rollo excitedly; "but he is coming back with a policeman. I wish Kizzy would come home. What shall we do?"

"He won't catch me," said Alf, with a little laugh and a catch in his breath.

"But I should let him come in, and then explain that you were trying to put the fire out," urged Rollo.

"Hark 'ee," said Alf impatiently. "When they comes back keep 'em waitin' as long as 'ee can. Tell 'em as many crams as 'ee can make up. Talk to 'em out o' the windy, an' tell 'em the key have stuck in the door, an' 'ee can't open 'un nohow wi'out a blacksmith. Then tell 'em that I be mortal bad, an' the doctor did say it might be small-pox. By'm by let 'em in very soft. They'll find me in bed sure enough!"

He gave a little chuckling laugh.

"But," said Rollo slowly, "I can't tell lies, Alf. I'll do anything else. I think I can manage him quite as well without lies. I'll do my very best for you. It's very exciting, isn't it?"

"Go on upstairs an' keep watch out o' the windy,"

said Alf gruffly, with difficulty suppressing a groan;
"this pain be cruel bad! 'Tis a cryin' shame to hound
a poor innercent lad out o' his sick-bed. Go on, will
'ee, don't crawl like a twoad!"

Rollo dashed upstairs obediently. He opened the
window, and waited patiently, but half an hour passed
by before any one appeared. Then, alas! it was not
Kizzy, but the farmer, with a policeman as stalwart and
strong as himself.

"Oh dear!" sighed poor Rollo. "I must do what a
policeman tells me, whatever it is. I daren't say 'No'
to him or I shall be put into prison. What shall I do?
If I don't speak to them I expect they will break the
door open."

For a moment he was quite paralysed, and gazed
down upon them with a white and speechless face.

The policeman looked up at him with a broad smile.

"Good arternoon, sir. Us must trouble you to open
the door. Be Keziah to home? Her be a real good
sort, an' 'twas a womanly thing to do arter all said an'
done. But gypsies be allays scoundrels. Come 'ee
down, sir, an' open the door perlite like."

"It isn't polite to come into Kizzy's house when she
is away," said Rollo, pursing up his mouth for a whistle,
a sign that he was "feeling a bit shaky."

Then a sudden inspiration seized him.

"Mr. Policeman, won't you go to her, and ask her
what you want to know? She went up to the Squire's to
take some eggs. I'm sure she would like that best
She told me the other day not to let any one in when
she was out. I remember she said that one day a
pedlar came, and he wasn't a pedlar at all; he was——"

"You come down this minit' or I'll give 'ee a good thrashin' when I sees 'ee ! " shouted the farmer.

Rollo's face looked very white and determined.

" I won't come down to be thrashed," he said ; and a spice of boyish mischief stole into his eyes. " I would rather stay up here, thank you. It would be much more comfortable."

" Come, young master," said the smiling policeman. " Us only does want a word wi' the chap that is ill. I makes so bold as to say that Mr. Ruttaway here may be mistaken, an' it ain't the feller he be looking for at all. Just one word wi' un will do the job. Us wouldn't be that cruel to drag a poor sick lad off his bed, an' take him off wi'out a word. Come 'ee down, sir, like a little gentleman, an' open the door to us, an' I'll see Mr. Ruttaway don't lay his finger on 'ee. 'Tis only his manner o' talking ! "

Rollo wavered, a little longer he parleyed, then very slowly and sadly descended the stairs.

" It's no good, Alf," he cried in a whisper ; " they're coming in, but I won't tell them where you are."

A minute after and he opened the door. The farmer marched in triumphantly, and seeing the kitchen was empty, went straight upstairs, calling to the policeman to follow him. He did so, and Rollo darted into the back kitchen.

" Alf ! " he whispered.

Alf was in bed again, his yellow handkerchief round his throat just showing above the sheet, but his head was hidden, and he lay as still as death."

" Oh, Alf, I'm so sorry. I couldn't keep them out."

Alf made no reply, and he ran out just as they came downstairs.

As a last resource Rollo stood in front of the farmer.

"You'll be sorry when you see how ill he is, and he didn't do it, he told me he didn't!"

"Where is the rascal?" asked the farmer. And with one stride he was in the back kitchen.

He paused when he saw the form under the bed-clothes.

"Be he shammin'? or be he very ill?"

Rollo did not answer. He was wondering at Alf's strange silence.

The policeman stepped up and spoke more gently.

"Come, my lad, this 'ere gent wants to have a word wi' yer. Lift up your head, and answer his questions."

"There be no questions that 'a be going to spake," said the farmer impatiently, " but 'a've seed wot 'a have comed here for, an' that be his yaller kerchief. What do you think o' this as a match now, policeman?"

He drew out of his pocket a scrap of yellow that was identically the same in colour and texture as that round Alf's throat.

The policeman bent over the bed with a puzzled look, then astonished Rollo by rapidly seizing hold of the bed clothes and turning them back.

The farmer uttered an angry oath.

A long broom, enveloped in blankets with the yellow handkerchief tied round its head, was the quiet occupant of Alf's bed.

And Alf had successfully made his escape. There was no sign of him anywhere.

CHAPTER XII

Miss Greening,
the Lodger

ROLLO was questioned and cross-questioned, but he was innocent of the trick which the farmer imputed at once to him. And happily Keziah's return shielded him from any more unpleasantness. She rounded on the farmer as a woman of her calibre could do, and finally he and the policeman walked away discomfited.

"What do I care for your hayricks? If the poor lad had been guilty of murder, is that a reason for you comin' an tryin' to drag him off a sick-bed, an' frighten him out of the house an' roof that has been shelterin' him these days? An' if he be found stone dead on the hard high-road, 'tis you, and the likes o' you, that have driven him to his death."

When they had gone Rollo turned breathlessly to her.

"Do you think he is really gone, Kizzy? It was very clever of him to do that. Don't you think he may be hiding somewhere?"

"No, I think he be well away from this part by now. The doctor said yesterday he would be soon on his legs again, but I didn't think how soon."

Kizzy gave a sigh, then dismissed him from her mind, and went out amongst her beloved fowls. A minute after she called out to Rollo—

" Where be your pony, sir ? "

" In the stable. I fed him just before the farmer came."

" He bain't there, nor yet in the orchard."

Rollo ran out. Dandy, and Dandy's saddle and bridle, had both disappeared. Keziah shook her head in dismay.

" That Alf has taken him; I fears he be no good at all! Small wonner they couldn't catch sight of him if he were on the pony's back. Now what shall I say to Mr. Lionel? What shall us do ? "

" But I'm sure Alf will bring it back, I'm sure he will. You see, he couldn't walk very well. He only borrowed it. Oh, I'm sure he is not a wicked boy. He wouldn't be a thief ! "

Keziah shook her head gloomily.

" Gypsies be trained to be thieves. They be born an' bred in horse stealin', an' fowl stealin', an' poachin', an' sich like. 'Tis their natur', they can't help theirsels. I'm sorry I left the house."

But Rollo stoutly defended his absent friend, and when Lionel appeared late that day, and the story was told to him, even his sceptism as to Alf's innocence did not shake the little boy's trust in the gypsy lad.

Lionel came back in bright spirits. He was vexed at Dandy's disappearance, and went to the police station the next day about it. He advertised his loss in a local paper, but it did not seem to trouble him as much as his old nurse feared it would do.

"He was only hired, and now I shall have to pay full price for him, and how to go on I know not!"

"Oh, do let me walk," pleaded Rollo. "I'm sure I could walk a lot more than I do. Do try me. I feel so strong and well, and I haven't had a headache for ages."

"Very well, you shall. We will do our tramp in very easy stages. After all it is only air and sunshine that we are seeking."

They left Keziah's the next day. She watched them depart very wistfully.

"Have you no news to tell your old nurse, Mr. Lionel?" she said, when the moment of parting had come.

He looked at her with a twinkle in his eye.

"Not yet, Kizzy, but I promise to write if I have any that would interest you."

"And Kizzy," said Rollo, as he put his small hand in hers, "give Alf my love when he brings my pony back. I'm quite sure he will. And tell him I'm looking out for him along the road."

She nodded and smiled to him, then went back to her lonely cottage and wiped a tear off her cheek with the corner of her apron.

"Bless his little trustin' heart. He don't doubt no one nor nothin', and hath that faith an' feelin' o' livin' wi' the Lord close to him, that it makes I right 'shamed of my wicked unbelief!"

Away through the little village walked uncle and nephew, climbing up hills very slowly, descending to cool shady lanes and a grey rushing river. They had a substantial lunch at a wayside inn, then began to ascend

a wide stretch of moor. The air grew cool and in-
vigorating. When they at last came to the level, and
saw miles of heather and granite, interspersed with
yellow gorse, and blue and purple tors in the distance,
Lionel bared his head and drew in a long, satisfied sigh.

"Now we will enjoy a rest," he announced. "We
will stay here for a couple of hours."

He cast himself down on the ground in the shade of
a pile of stones. Rollo sat down contentedly by his
side.

"I s'pose you'll have a smoke and a sleep," he said.

"I don't know about sleep," said Lionel, as he lazily
filled his pipe; "do you object?"

"I would like a little talk," said Rollo modestly.

"Talk, you voracious youngster? What else have
we been doing for the six or seven hours we have spent
already of this day?"

"Yes, but that has been of things we were passing,"
said Rollo, wrinkling his brow. "I want a real talk
now."

"I will give you twenty minutes! Fire ahead!"

"I was wondering about Alf. I wish I had said
goodbye to him. I hoped you would have come back
and given him a message. I think he would have
liked one."

"Couldn't you have given him one?"

"No," said Rollo doubtfully. "I shouldn't have
known what to say. He laughed when I said things
sometimes. I remember you said every one we met
ought to give us a message or get one. I would rather
get messages than give them. I'm too small to be a
messenger."

"We aren't told how old Samuel was, but I fancy he was rather a small chap," said Lionel slowly.

"And then I don't carry any about with me," said Rollo.

"No, and I won't give you any of mine. I don't want to turn you into a man before your time. You would be better for a little less meditation and more play; that is the disadvantage of being in my company so much. Don't bother your head about messages. Let your life tell whose you are and whom you serve. And if your heart is filled as it ought to be, it will overflow, and the parched ground will be so much the better for the droppings."

Lionel did not often "preach," but every word he uttered was treasured up by his small nephew, who pondered over many things. He lay down on the heather now, and watched the larks and bees and butterflies as they passed to and fro. Presently he spoke again.

"You know our book that we're going to write?"

"Any more ideas?"

"Yes," Rollo said slowly; "I think we must have a chapter about 'love.'"

Lionel almost dropped his pipe out of his mouth with the sudden start he gave. But he recovered himself in an instant.

"A very large theme. Universal love, perhaps? Love of our Creator, our race, our brother-man?"

Rollo brought his wonderful blue eyes steadily upon his uncle's face.

"No," he said simply; "Kizzy and I were talking it over in her orchard. She said it was the way young men were took—she called it a long name—an epi, something."

" Upon my word, you're beginning early.   Go on, and tell me more of this interesting conversation."

" It comes to people before they get married, Kizzy said, and she said sometimes it was bad for people and sometimes it was good for them.   She made it out very nice on the whole, I think, but I waited till I could talk it over with you, for I knew you would explain it best."

Lionel looked away over the heather in silence for a minute.

"Yes, we must have a chapter on love," he said, a little dreamily.   " Love is to life what poetry is to prose, what the sunshine is to flowers, what the spring is to the hard, dry, budding trees.   It is the one bit of Eden that God has left in the world, and that can be kept pure and sweet and good."

Then Rollo came to business.

" Would you rather have *her* with you than me ? "

Lionel looked at the boy sternly.

"I don't think you mean to be impertinent," he said.

" Oh ! indeed I don't ! " was Rollo's quick response. "But I told Kizzy about her, and we thought—at least I did—that you might be getting tired of me. I don't want you to be, and she looked so beautiful, and—please don't look at me like that, I don't mean to be rude—but I do want to know all about her."

" You want to know a great deal too much," was the crushing reply.

Rollo's head drooped. He was silent. With the strange inconsistency that sometimes seizes a young man, Lionel was a few minutes afterwards giving his nephew a full account of his lady love, her family, her circumstances, and last, but not least, her perfections. The boy listened with eager interest.   It sounded like a fairy tale to him.   And Lionel, under the glamour of the moorland air and sunshine, the still lovely loneliness of heather toes, and the fresh, sweet sympathy of a child, spoke out of his heart's depths, and left the indelible impression upon his nephew's brain that love—true love —was the pivot on which the whole wide world was turned.

Time slipped by, and shadows began to creep across the blue tors.

Lionel roused himself.

"We must be walking on," he said; "we have two miles of heather, and then there is our farmhouse where I want to stop the night."

So away they trudged, the fresh moor breeze exhilarating and quickening their steps.

"I think I can walk better than ride," said Rollo.   "I don't feel a bit tired."

But he was glad enough when the farmhouse was reached.

"I have heard you take lodgers," Lionel said when the door was opened by a rosy-cheeked young woman. "Can you find room for us to-night?"

"Oh, yes, sir," she responded.   "We have no one with us at present except an old lady.   Would you like to see the rooms that are vacant?"

The farmhouse had originally been an old manor. The entrance was a lofty, stone-flagged hall, with an oak staircase at the farther end.   She opened one of the

many rooms that led out of this, and they found themselves in an old oak wainscoted room with deep window
seats, and a large square table in the centre of it. The
furniture looked poor and meagre in the handsome
room, but everything was clean and neat. An old-
fashioned sideboard, a horsehair sofa, six chairs ranged
with their backs against the wall, and two armchairs,
were all that was in it.

Lionel walked to the window and looked out, then
ordered tea; and Rollo curled himself up on the
sofa.

"I do like this," he remarked; "we haven't been in a
house like this before, have we? Do you think I could
go all over it after tea?"

"I dare say," replied Lionel absently.

Their meal was a substantial one. The farmer's wife
sent them in a large dish of broiled trout freshly caught
in the river that day; boiled eggs, cold ham, honey, a
dish of watercress, and a large currant loaf also graced
their board, besides a plentiful supply of bread and
butter and cream.

When it was over Lionel sauntered out into the
garden. Rollo ran upstairs to look at their bedrooms.

He had a dressing-room opening out of a large one.
There was a long corridor with rooms on each side, and
he peeped into several, with boyish curiosity. But as
his head was round the corner of one he was startled by
a voice.

"Now, little boy, what are you doing here? Do you
know that you are peeping into my room?"

He turned round and saw behind him a tall old lady
in a very large mushroom hat and yellow leather gloves.

"I beg your pardon," he said confusedly. "I've only just come, and I was looking about me."

"I don't suppose my room is different to your own, but you can come in if you like. Come in, and wipe your shoes on the mat. I have been into the garden, and have been driven in by a man's pipe. Does he belong to you? Ah, my dear, don't you ever smoke, it is an uncleanly, pernicious habit, and I'm quite sure Adam wouldn't have been allowed to do so in the garden of Eden. If he was happy without it, why shouldn't the young men of to-day be the same?"

Rollo did not know what to say, but he fell in love with the old lady on the spot, and looked about her quaint room with the greatest of interest. A little fire burned in the grate, and though it was in the height of summer it did not seem out of place, for the sun had gone down, and the room was a large one. A Persian cat lay before the fire, and in one of the large windows was a cage with two small owls. There was an easel with an unfinished painting upon it, and the rest of the room was littered with books and papers.

Newspapers seemed to be on every chair in the room, and there was a great pile of them on the floor behind the door.

The old lady went to a cupboard.

"Don't think I am Old Mother Hubbard," she said, with a twinkle in her eye, "because I have got a cupboard. I have some cake here, and boys always like cake. Now, sit down on that chair, don't make crumbs, and tell me who you are."

Rollo promptly obeyed, and she stood looking at him as he spoke, with her hands resting on her hips.

I

"Dear me, how unique! Now, why cannot I manage
to find some one to tramp with? I should dearly like
to see the country, and then I should come home and
write a book upon it."

"That's what we mean to do," Rollo said confidentially ; "do you write books?"

"There is nothing," said the old lady, with a little
laugh, "that I don't attempt to do. I paint, I write, I
work I garden, I botanise, I read, and a host of other
things besides. I had a mother once, and she was the
only one of seven sisters who died a happy old woman.
She had a full life and she gloried in it. She lived for
others, her sisters lived for themselves. They were
wretched, in body, soul, and spirit, and died as they
lived. Now I am quite alone and I haven't a relation
in the world, and yet I mustn't say that, for I look upon
the whole human race as my sisters and brothers. I try
to work for those that cannot work for themselves.
What are you doing in that way?"

Rollo looked startled.

"I'm afraid I don't quite understand," he said.

"Are you living for self or for others?"

"I s'pose I'm living because God wants me to," said
Rollo, with a wrinkled brow.

The old lady smiled.

"Ah well," she said, "we mustn't expect old heads
on young shoulders. You have to grow at present, and
that's a trying process sometimes."

"But I can't make myself grow," said Rollo wonderingly.

"You can obey the laws for growth. Take exercise,
good food, and inhale pure air, and if you do the same

for your soul as for your body, your inner and outer man will prosper."

Rollo thought this was strange talk, but he was interested.

"It's funny about growing," he said meditatively. "You never see it being done, but I s'pose you always grow when you're asleep. The flowers never move all day, for I've watched them, and yet they get bigger and bigger, and puppies and kittens are just the same. They grow into dogs and cats, and yet you never see them doing it."

The old lady nodded.

"It's just the same with your inner man. It is the same silent growth, and the person who ought to know least about it is yourself."

"Why?" asked Rollo.

"Because we have naturally such a lot of pride and self-conceit about us that the less we think about ourselves the better."

"You have quite done growing," said Rollo, looking at his new friend with great respect.

"My body has done growing, and is doing the other thing at present."

"What is that?"

"Shrinking, to be sure. Many old people get smaller as they get older, but I hope I'm still growing in other ways."

"And how do you give your soul food?" asked Rollo.

The old lady put her hand reverently on a Bible that was near her. "This is my pantry or storehouse," she said quaintly. "I find plain, wholesome food, exhilarating tonics, and medicine when I require it. Sweets and bitters, but all making and helping growth."

"And you said exercise."

"Yes, I did. You must use your body if you want it to work well. You must exercise faith and trust and love and hope if your soul is to grow. Those are its limbs. Faith and obedience, the hands. One to take, one to act. Trust and belief, the feet—standing firm on the right foundation. Hope, the eyes; love, the heart and mouth."

"That sounds very difficult," murmured Rollo. "And do you give your soul pure air?"

"Ah, the question of atmosphere is a most important one."

The old lady paused, then put her head out of the window, and looked up into the blue sky. "Nothing and no one between you and the sun," she said solemnly, when she drew her head back. "Now, is there anything else you would like to know?"

"No, thank you," said Rollo slowly. "I think I had better go back to my uncle."

CHAPTER XIII

The Highwayman

ROLLO heard a little more about their fellow lodger from the farmer's wife, who came up to see him when he was in bed.

"I always do think," she said, after asking him if he was quite comfortable, "that a boy do want a woman to look to him. My boys do, an' you be very small to go about by yoursel'. Miss Greening, our lady lodger, her said to me just now, 'Mrs. Williams,' her said, 'look well to the wants of the little fellow, his head works very fast for its size.'"

"Tell me about Miss Greening," said Rollo, who always felt guilty of something wrong when his head was discussed, though he did not quite see where the fault lay.

"Her be a very good woman, Miss Greening be, though rayther peculiar. I reckon that her have plenty o' money, but her gives it all away. Her selleth her bits o' paintin's, an' sendeth it to orphans an' such like. Her doth beeutiful bits o' needlework, but it do all get sent away to needy families; her sendeth her flowers up to London hospitals; an' did you see all her newspapers? Her be a great reader; but if her seeth in 'em a sad accident, an' widder an' orphans left, her goeth straight to post-office an' sendeth off a bit o' money to the parson of their parish for 'em. Her be a wonnerful charitable lady."

"I should like to stay here several days," said Rollo the next morning at breakfast.

Lionel did not answer him for a minute or two. He was absorbed in a letter. Rollo eyed it in dismay, for there were several closely written sheets, and he was longing to talk.

At last, with a smile, Lionel put it into his pocket and spoke.

"Did you say you wanted to stay longer here? We can't do that. As it is, we are taking very easy marches. We shall still have a bit of moor to walk over to-day, so we will start early, for there will be no shade and we shall find it very warm."

"Do you think I might go upstairs and wish Miss Greening goodbye?"

"Is that your friend of last night? Be quick, then, while I pay my bill, and then we must be off."

Rollo dashed upstairs, and knocked very gently at Miss Greening's door. There was no answer, and after waiting some minutes he opened the door very quietly. There was no one there, and he rejoined Lionel with a troubled look on his face.

"I can't find her. I don't like tramping in a hurry. I hadn't finished knowing her."

"How long does that take?" asked his uncle.

"Well, I always take one day to begin. Some people are quick to know. I'm sure I should have finished her in a few days."

"Very flattering," said a voice behind. He was

standing talking to Lionel on the stone terrace outside
the hall door, and turning quickly he saw Miss Greening
with her hands full of roses close to him.

The pink colour came into his cheeks, but he was not
aware he had said anything peculiar.

He put out his small hand.

"I did want to say goodbye to you," he said. "We
are going away, that is the worst of being tramps—you
have to say goodbye to somebody every day."

She astonished him by stooping down and kissing him.

"Don't forget to grow," she said. "Remember—
food, air, exercise! God bless you!"

She went indoors, and, with a wistful look after her,
Rollo followed his uncle down the drive and out on the
moor.

Their walk was a quiet one that morning. They
stopped to have their lunch by the side of a small
stream. Lionel sat down and began to write, and Rollo
amused himself by taking off his shoes and stockings
and wading in the stream. After an hour's rest they
started again, and were soon following a winding hilly
lane that wound up and down in a most bewildering
manner. The air seemed close and sultry, heavy
clouds rolled up, and soon distant rumbles of thunder
proclaimed a coming storm. They hastened their steps,
and to Lionel's relief they came to the inn which was
their goal before the storm burst upon them.

In a dingy parlour Rollo knelt on a chair by the
window, and watched the lightning play on the distant
hills. Dark masses of cloud seemed to roll backwards
and forwards, and the claps of thunder were loud and
incessant.

He had no fear in watching it, and at last turned round to Lionel, who was deep in his favourite map.

"I used to think," he remarked, "that lightning was a chink into heaven, just a hole through, you know, which would show you things if it only stayed long enough ; I suppose it isn't, but I should like to be closer up to it all. In a balloon it would be grand !"

"There wouldn't be much of you left if you were," said Lionel drily.

Rollo left the window and curled himself up in an easy chair.

"Can we have a talk ?" he asked.

"Go ahead."

"I haven't had time to tell you yet what Miss Greening said to me. I thought if we talked it out we could put it into our book."

"What's the subject ?"

"Growing."

"Humph !"

"Everybody growing," said Rollo hastily, "and growing inside and out, and doing things to make yourself grow, and then not wanting to find out whether you're big or little, but letting other people do that."

"That sounds sensible," said Lionel drily. "Go on."

"You must never expect to see your soul grow any more than you do your body," went on Rollo, with the far-away look in his eyes that his uncle loved to see there. "Do you think we grow as fast inside as out ?"

"I think you do," responded his uncle, with a smile. "Some people's souls don't grow at all. And some shrink away to nothing. I believe bodies hinder souls from growing a great deal."

"I s'pose," said Rollo gravely, "you don't have to grow any more when you get to heaven. Everything is finished there."

"Not at all," said his uncle. "I think we shall all do a lot of growing there. It is only the beginning of knowledge that we get in this life."

"I think we might have a lot about flowers growing and animals, as well as people, in our chapter; shall we?"

"Evolution," muttered Lionel. The long word was lost upon Rollo.

"And Miss Greening said we must eat and drink with our souls, and give them exercise and good air."

Talk was interrupted by their evening meal appearing, and Rollo's thoughts became engrossed in supplying the needs of his body.

The storm went on at intervals till bedtime came. As Rollo was going up the narrow little staircase leading to his room, he was startled by seeing the figure of a girl crouched down in a corner, sobs shaking her frame.

"What's the matter?" he asked.

"Oh," sobbed the girl, raising a frightened, tear-stained, and rather grimy face; "I be so wisht and scared, I be fit to die. This thunder do praperly shake me innerds all to pieces, an' now it be dark, it be terrible!"

"Are you frightened of the storm? Why don't you go to your mother?"

"I have no mother, nor nothin'; I be missus's maid, an' I be workin' in the kitchen from morn to night. Missus be cruel to me, her pulled out the knives I did hide away, an' her laughed, an' sent me to bed when I cried."

"Why are you frightened?" asked Rollo.

"Oh, I be dreadful scared! It will kill me like it did my aunt's cousin! Her were found wi' her face all black an' streaky a-sittin' on a wooden bench, just as her had satted down, an' her 'brella were split into fifty bits o' ribbon!"

She gave a little stifled shriek as a flash of lightning illumined her hiding-place.

"I think you'd better ask God to take care of you, and then you needn't be frightened," said Rollo, looking at her thoughtfully. "Of course it isn't very nice to be killed, and have your face black and streaky, but I don't think that happens to many people. Tell God you would rather not die that way, and I'm quite sure He'll manage that you don't!"

The girl stared at him.

Rollo went on, earnestly determined to comfort her—

"I'm not afraid of storms, I like them; but there's one thing that I don't like to think of, and that is of being burnt up in a fire. I've seen fires in London, and there was a boy our cook knew who was burnt to a cinder. It must be so dreadfully painful. I've asked God to be so good as to see that I don't get killed that way, and I'm quite positive certain that He won't let me be."

"I can't make a prayer," admitted the poor girl, though a gleam of light and hope came to her dull blue eyes.

"Oh, yes you can. It's only speaking. And you needn't speak out loud."

"But God won't listen to the likes o' me."

"He hears everybody who speaks to Him, and He always answers. Make haste and pray to Him, and then you'll feel all right."

The girl shook her head, then Rollo knelt down by her.

"Please, God, don't kill this girl in a thunderstorm. She doesn't like it, and keep her from being frightened, and take care of her. For Jesus Christ's sake. Amen."

When he had left off speaking the girl took up his prayer and repeated it word for word with an awestruck face.

There was a minute's silence, then Rollo said conclusively—

"There! You need never be frightened any more, because if God is taking care of you, no thunder or lightning would dare to touch you. Good-night."

He ran off to bed, and the girl crept off to hers with an indescribable feeling of comfort and relief.

"He do seem so certain sure that it must be true," she said, and she fell asleep in peace.

The next morning was a lovely one. They were off on their travels early, but their journey was uneventful, mostly through lanes and by-ways. They stopped at a good-sized town in the middle of the day, then pushed on, and found themselves as evening drew near crossing a wild bit of moorland. There was a little rough sheep track which they were following, but a heavy mist began to roll across the moor, and Lionel felt doubtful as to whether they had better proceed. He was making his way to an inn marked on his map, but they had still nearly two miles to go; and at length he stood still to consider.

"Hark!" said Rollo eagerly. "There's some one calling; don't you hear them?"

Very faintly but clearly a voice came to them through the mist—

" Help ! help ! help !   I'm lost !   Help ! "

" Stay where you are, Rollo, or we shall lose each
other.   I will light my lantern and give it to you.   Then
I shall be able to find the path again.   Don't move, I
must try and help this person."

Rollo was left alone, sturdily grasping his lantern, and
wondering if they were going to have a third companion
in their wanderings.

Suddenly he gave a violent start.   A man sprang out
of the mist apparently right in front of him.

" Yer money or yer life ! " he shouted loudly as he
levelled a pistol full in Rollo's face.   He wore a black
mask, and now that an actual highwayman stood before
him, Rollo did not find the experience so pleasant as he
had always imagined it would be.

" I've only fivepence halfpenny," he said, trying to
speak manfully, and wondering if he would be a coward
if he did not at once fight this outlaw.   He had no time
for reflection.   His lantern was dashed from his hand,
a heavy cloak thrown over his head, and then he felt
himself picked up as if he had been a baby and slung
across the man's shoulder.   He breathed with difficulty,
and struggle as he did, his captor seemed strong enough
to be indifferent to his efforts.

It seemed a very long time before he was put down
on his feet.   When the cloak was taken from him, he
found himself in a little dark hollow in a wood, a blazing
fire, a queer-looking tent, and three or four very rough-
looking men completed the picture.   The men were
eating their supper, and a pot was boiling merrily,
suspended over the fire, out of which they helped themselves by means of forked sticks.

Rollo looked about him in a dazed fashion. Was this a highwayman's haunt? A bandit's cave? And where was his captor? He had disappeared, but the oldest of the men addressed him.

"Sit down, youngster. Do 'ee think us be goin' to eat yer?"

"I hope I don't look frightened," said Rollo, standing with his legs well apart and his hands in his pockets. "Because I'm not frightened of you," he went on with quivering emphasis; "not one bit."

A laugh came from them, then one of the men put out his hand and drew him to him.

"Don't 'ee crow too loud, young cock. Fork out that there watch o' yourn an' be quick."

Rollo's cheeks were very white, but his hands never moved from his pockets.

"Mother sent me that on my last birthday," he said. "I wouldn't think of giving it away. It would be wicked if you stole it, for I could never get another like it."

The man put his great hand in at the back of his neck and gave him a little shake. Rollo was dizzy for a minute, then when he looked down he was minus his watch and chain, and the contents of his pockets were cleared completely out. The man lay back and laughed at his scared face.

"Us don't take much longer to shake the breath out of a youngster's body if he give us any tongue," he said, "an' then the pot be glad to receive his little body, an' us have an extra good stew the nex' night."

The broad wink of the others that accompanied these words somewhat reassured Rollo. But he judged silence was discretion.

"Where be that young fool off to?" asked another of
the men. "What do he want us to do wi' the kid?"

There was no answer. Rollo stood irresolute before
them for a minute, then his courage returned to
him.

"I think," he said in his old-fashioned way, "that I
might sit down and have a little of your supper. I'm
hungry. And then if you don't mind I should like to
spend the night with you, and when this mist has gone
away in the morning I expect you'll let me go, and I
must try to find my uncle."

One of the men laughed, but on the whole they
seemed good-natured, and soon Rollo was sitting
amongst them sharing their meal, and fast losing his first
dread of them.

Their talk was for the most part inexplicable to him,
for so many words and phrases they used were unknown
to him, but he entertained them by his remarks and questions, and after a time his head began to nod, and his
eyes to droop. One of the men had pity on him, and
lifted him inside the tent, throwing an old coat over him,
and there Rollo slept soundly till he was awakened by a
voice in his ear.

"Get up—don't 'ee make a noise—an' foller me."

Rollo tried to obey, but he was sleepy, and his legs
were stiff. He felt himself being picked up and carried
away into the open. A few minutes after he found
himself being placed on a pony's back, and then he
uttered a little scream of surprise and joy, for Dandy was
underneath him, and Alf was by his side.

CHAPTER XIV

By the Sea

"OH, Alf, Alf! I'm so glad to see you! Do tell me how you found me here."

"Hist! Not so much noise. I'll tell 'ee fast enough."

It was barely light. A line of silver crossed the horizon of the moor; the mist had gone, and Alf was carefully and quietly leading Dandy through a little dell of thick bushes and trees.

"Did yer like the highwayman?" Alf inquired; "didn't he do it praper? Same as us talked about 'un when I were abed!"

Rollo began to understand.

"You've been playing me a trick," he said, with a radiant face. "I believe you dressed up and carried me away! Of course you did, and that was your gypsy camp last night! I thought it wasn't quite like a highwayman's place!"

"A lot better," said Alf hastily. "I have bin preparin' this little adventure for yer ever since I bolted."

"How very good of you! I really have enjoyed it!"

There was a little hesitation in Rollo's voice, and Alf laughed outright.

"'Ee did look praper scared, but now 'ee knows what it be like."

"Yes, I do," assented Rollo, with laborious cheerfulness, "but I think next time—if it ever happens again—I should like to be quite sure that it's only fun!"

Alf shook his head. "No, that 'ud spile the whole bus'ness. 'Ow's the old woman? Tell us what that there old bloke looked like when he got hold o' my yaller handkerchy!"

Rollo gave a detailed account of all that had occurred since Alf had departed, which the delinquent much enjoyed, as his frequent delighted chuckles testified.

"But how," asked Rollo in bewilderment, "did you find me last night?"

"Wall," said Alf, "'ow did ye find me? I have just done 'ee the same good turn 'ee did for me. I picked 'ee up, an' am puttin' ee on the pony, an' as to findin' of 'ee, bless 'ee, I've had my eye on 'ee an' on yer gent ever since I left 'ee. I was only waitin' my time."

"I s'pose," said Rollo thoughtfully, "that taking my watch was only fun. I haven't got it back."

Alf put his hand in his pocket and drew it out. "Ye had better clear off now, for some o' our chaps is gone on yer pony; don't 'ee come this way agen. I'll tell 'em 'ow ye stole off unbeknownst to I. 'Twas a clever way to giv' ye the pony back agen, an' yer watch was just a mistake. The chap that took it didn't know me as he oughted to!"

Rollo looked perplexed.

"You won't tell a story, Alf, about the pony?"

Alf laughed.

"'Tis getting light; see that little 'ouse by the trees

there ? That be the nearest inn. Ye be sure to find yer uncle there."

"I don't know," said Rollo; "perhaps I shan't. He went away from me to help some one else who was lost."

Again Alf laughed.

"Ye be such a innercent! 'Twas I set up that screechin' to get the gent off yer trac'!"

Rollo looked at him in wonder.

"An' now," pursued Alf, "I'll say good-day, an' thank 'ee kindly for givin' of me that nussin'; that did me a world o' good, an' if 'ee'd like another taste o' robbin' at night, I'll do it different nex' time!"

"Oh no, thank you! I think I won't have another adventure just yet."

Rollo's tone was emphatic; then he looked at the gypsy lad rather wistfully.

"I think if we're saying goodbye I'd like to do what my uncle does and give you a message. He has little books that he gives away. But I haven't any, only the day you left, Alf, I wrote out something on paper to give you when I saw you next. I knew you would bring back Dandy. Would you like to have it ? It's a—a text out of the Bible, because my uncle's books all come out of the Bible."

Rollo felt very carefully in his pocket. The slip of paper was still there, and had not tumbled out with his other possessions.

He opened it, and read it out to Alf, who looked at it with mingled feelings of amusement and dismay—

"For the ways of man are before the eyes of the Lord, and He pondereth all his goings."

"It's what mother wrote in my Bible," said Rollo;

K

"she said in a letter to me that it was a good thing to remember when I was going to do naughty things, so I thought you might like it too. You're more of a man than I am, Alf, but I hope to be growing up soon."

Alf took the paper and put it into one of his pockets. "I'll read it on a Sunday," he said. "Goodbye, little 'un!"

He dashed back into the wood, and was seen no more. Rollo rode slowly on, thinking of many things. He was not anxious about his uncle, as he felt confident that he would meet him at the inn, but when he arrived there, the landlord informed him that a "gent with two men" had been searching the moor all night for a lost child. "An' he be just come in, an' have gone up for a wash, bein' praperly wored out!"

Rollo got off his pony and ran up the little stairs to the room indicated. Lionel received him with a long-drawn breath of relief.

But he did not view Alf's proceedings in the same grateful light that his nephew did, and Rollo was puzzled at his wrath.

"Alf planned it all out to please me, he really did," the boy urged, when Lionel declared he ought to be in gaol. "He only kept Dandy till he made himself into a highwayman. We used to talk about it, and I said how very nice it would be to have an adventure. You see, the days are rather quiet, and I thought it would keep you and me from feeling dull. Alf wouldn't have done it if he hadn't known I wanted it, and he has taken great care of Dandy. Please don't be angry with him!"

Lionel began to see the humorous side of it.

"I should be glad," he said in his dry manner, "if you would notify to me next time any adventure of this sort that you have been planning. I am sorry you find the days so dull, but I do not find wandering about in a moor mist all night so very exhilarating!"

"I think," admitted Rollo slowly, "that stories of adventure are nicer than when you have them in real life. I won't wish for it again, I promise you!"

Breakfast was a silent meal. After it was over Lionel went off to a little trout stream near to fish. He left Rollo in the small inn parlour to rest, for he looked fagged and white.

"I had better write my letter to mother," Rollo said, "I shall have plenty to tell her to-day."

So he was left with pen and ink and paper, and for some time he found his employment sufficiently engrossing to occupy his time and thoughts. But the letter was finished at last, and then he wandered about the room disconsolately.

"I have been told to stay in, so I must stay in," he soliloquised, "but I really must find some one to talk to."

He put his head out of the window, and to his joy saw the landlord, a jovial-looking man, digging up some potatoes in a piece of ground close to the house.

A conversation was started at once. Rollo gave a full and particular account of his adventure, to which the landlord listened with open mouth and eyes.

"Them gypsies be a bad lot," he remarked. "They getteth a livin' wi'out puttin' they hands to work, which is in course contrary to right an' Scriptur'. Some on 'em do make a purtence o' mendin' an' tinkerin' pots an' pans, an' there be a bit o' basket work done by others, but the most part be idle vagabon's, a-stealin' an' poachin' an' trickin' on honest folks' grounds."

"I like them," Rollo said stoutly—"at least I liked Alf; but is it wicked to live without working, because I think I'm doing it."

"I broughted up my boys to work sin' they could put out their han's an' feet. Idleness makes more rogues an' thieves than ought else that I knows of."

"I shall work when I grow up, of course," said Rollo hastily. "I am not quite sure what I shall do. I change my mind so often, but I shan't work in London. I shall come to the country. Do you think I could keep an inn like you? It doesn't seem very difficult, and I should like to put up tramps like us and talk to them. Don't you like seeing new people? I do, only the worst of it is, we never seem to see them again. There's one thing, I shall have a lot of people to talk to when I get to heaven and see them there. And we *must* see everybody on the Judgment Day!"

The landlord rubbed his head.

"Ay, little master, ye have a wunnerful tongue," was all that he found to say, but when Lionel returned to a midday meal, he found an animated conversation going on between them on the merits and demerits of class distinction.

"I sometimes wonder if Miss Percy trains you to talk," Lionel remarked, as they were consuming a beefsteak together. "Now what on earth have you to say about such subjects?"

"He began it," said Rollo, hanging his head. "He made me feel it was wicked to be born rich. He said the Bible said so, but I told him lots of the good people were rich. Abraham, and Jacob, and Joseph. He said Jacob worked for his living; but he only did it while he was waiting to be married, didn't he? And then we were wondering what the world would be if everybody was poor, all round, you know, and the king had to dig up potatoes for his dinner, but he said if everybody had equal, they would be rich then ; that was what it ought to be, so then I reminded him he said it was wicked to be rich, and then we got so confused that we couldn't get straight again."

"Well, now you can give your tongue a rest. Make a good dinner, for we must be starting at two o'clock. As you will be riding again, we can push on to a town I want to reach to-night."

At two o'clock they started. The landlord and one or two idle men gathered round the door to see them depart.

Rollo took off his hat and waved to them.

"Goodbye," he shouted to the landlord ; "goodbye— till the judgment day! I shall be sure to see you again then!"

With this startling assertion he rode away, and the landlord turned into the house, rubbing his head reflectively. He had one of Lionel's little books in his pocket. Was it mere coincidence that as he took it out the title stared him in the face : "So then every one of us shall give account of himself to God"?

And the messengers were moving on through the shady lanes ; the elder so absorbed in his thoughts that for the time being he was quite oblivious of the outer world; the younger noting with quick, eager glances every bird on the wing, every flower by the wayside, and delighting in every fresh object that Nature brought before him.

A few days later found them no longer in leafy lanes, or on a heather and bracken covered moor, but by the side of the grand old ocean, and Rollo's cup of happiness was full.

"Oh, do let us stay here for a week at least," he pleaded. "I have hardly ever been by the sea, and I have never seen such beautiful blue and green water, or such lovely seaweedy rocks."

They were in a quiet little fishing village, and had taken rooms in a small cottage facing the sea. Lionel was content to stay a time, so Rollo found his request granted at once. The weather was exquisite. At seven o'clock Rollo went out with his uncle to bathe. Eight o'clock breakfast followed, and for the rest of the day he was left pretty much to his own devices.

Of course he made friends with the fishermen, and before three days had passed, knew them all by name, and the various particulars of their respective homes and families.

Two other strangers were also lodging in the village. One was a thin gaunt old man, who was wheeled down to the beach every morning in a bath-chair, his servant attending to his wants with a devotion that was quite striking. The other was an artist, who perched his easel amongst a certain group of rocks, and painted away with untiring diligence till the sun began to set.

Rollo watched him with great awe and respect, and soon was on speaking terms with him.

"Has any one ever been able to paint the sun?" he asked one morning, as he stood watching the artist putting lines of broken light on the ripple of the waves.

The artist shook his head.

"We can paint different effects of the sun; we can depict him when he is shrouded in fog or mist, or in the act of rising or setting, but in his midday splendour he is an impossible subject."

"I s'pose," said Rollo slowly, "he is like God—too bright for our eyes."

Then after a pause he added—

"Pictures are funny things, aren't they? I feel I should like to walk right into your picture and put my legs into the sea that you've made, but there's one thing your paint doesn't do. It doesn't give it the proper smell. I wonder if you rubbed some seaweed over it, or washed it very carefully with a little sea, whether it would be better."

The artist smiled.

"Come now, small critic," he said, "paint a picture yourself, and then you will have scope to carry out all these original ideas of yours."

Rollo took the hint, and was forthwith smitten with a desire to paint. The artist good-naturedly lent him some little bits of paint, and he brought a camp stool out with great importance, and started work. But, alas! all his efforts were fruitless, and after several vain attempts, Rollo sorrowfully tore up his bit of paper.

"I can't do it, and I feel I should never learn. I s'pose I am too stupid."

"You cannot expect to do in one minute what has taken me years of hard grinding work to produce," said the artist.

Rollo took this to heart.

"But there's one thing I can do," he said brightly. "I can shut my eyes when I'm away from a thing, and I see it all there still. And sometimes when I'm in bed I shut my eyes and see all kinds of things—dragons and robbers, and birds' nests and gypsies, and the sun, and the flowers and the trees.   That is next best to painting them, isn't it ? "

"Certainly," assented the artist.

Then Rollo wandered away to make friends with the gentleman in the bath-chair, Mr. Smith-Tomkins by name.

He found conversation difficult with him, for he was a gloomy miserable man.   But occasionally Rollo's remarks drew him out of himself.

"After all," the small boy said by way of comfort, "it doesn't matter if your head is right, what your arms and legs are like, does it ?   I mean, your arms and legs don't think for you, or pretend.   I think pretending is very nice when you aren't well.   When I have a head-ache I try sometimes to pretend I'm in delicious places with no headache at all.   You know how hot and thirsty you get when your head is bad.   Well, I think of a stream pouring out through ferns and flowers in front of me, and a stream by my feet which I can put them into, if I want to, and then I pretend a black slave is fanning me on one side, and another is pouring out some iced lemonade, and then if I want to feel quite delicious I pretend mother is standing by me, and putting her hand on my forehead.   I think of her silk dress and her soft voice, and a smell like a rose about her, and then I make her say, 'Now, Rollo, you will feel better,' and generally when I get to that part I fall asleep, and don't feel my headache any more.   I wish you would try that when you feel rather ill."

A smile crossed the face of the invalid.

"No," he said, "the gift of imagination is not mine, only bitter memories."

"But you can remember some nice things," urged

Rollo. "When you were a boy like me, and had a mother, and the first time you went to the seaside."

"I was born by the sea," the gentleman said gloomily; "that is why I have come back to it. It is a restless, turbulent spirit like my own that cannot be calmed by time."

"I s'pose," said Rollo thoughtfully, "you would like to be tramping along like us, but the sea is quite calm sometimes."

"And so am I," said his friend impatiently; "as quiet and torpid as any sleeping toad or tortoise. My body is forced to be so, worse luck for me."

It was strange what confidences passed between the two. Lionel could get no talk at all from the sick man, but his small nephew seemed to enjoy his conversations with him thoroughly, and Mr. Smith-Tomkins' eyes had a wistful searching look in them if, when he was wheeled down to the beach, Rollo was not near at hand.

"Sims, his servant, has told me all about him," said Rollo one evening, as he and his uncle were partaking of a late supper together. "He said he used to hunt, and had a horse that was a bit of himself, and then he got a fall, and has never been able to walk since. And he was going to be married, and when he came a cripple, the lady married some one else. I think it was too bad of her, don't you? And Sims says he doesn't like to look at the country, and if he sees a fox he is awfully angry, and he likes looking out at the sea and nothing else."

"Poor fellow!" said Lionel sympathisingly. "What a trial! No wonder he looks so miserable."

"But he can read books," Rollo said enthusiastically; "he never has to be told that he mustn't do it. And he has money enough to buy every book that is ever written."

CHAPTER XV

Mr. Smith-Tomkins

IT was the last day of their stay at the sea, and Rollo was saying goodbye to his various friends. He had fished with one old man, shrimped with another, been out for a row with another, and there was hardly an inhabitant of the village to whom he had not talked.

"When I grow up," he informed a little group of them, "I promise you I will come back to this village, for I like it quite the best of all the places I have seen, and there is enough to make me busy, and keep me doing different things till I'm a hundred years old!"

The artist was sitting on his rocks when he went to bid him farewell.

"Goodbye, little tramp," he said; "you have an artist's soul if you have not an artist's fingers. There are different kinds of pictures remember. Canvas and paint do not produce the best sort, it may be the most lucrative. There are word pictures that appeal to hearts instead of eyes. There are thought pictures that make the unseen real and near to us. Paint away with your brain, and let others have the benefit of it."

Rollo left him with a grave thoughtful face, and went in search of Mr. Smith-Tomkins. He found him alone at the extremity of the beach, round a projecting cliff, and out of sight of the fishing boats and village. For a wonder his servant was not with him. He was sitting in his chair, a book on his knees; but his restless miserable eyes were roving over the ocean in front of him.

He turned, hearing the light footsteps approaching him, and a light leaped into his eyes.

"I have come to say goodbye," said Rollo, laying his little hand lightly on the worn wrinkle done. "It's the only disagreeable thing about tramping, having to say such hundreds of goodbyes."

"Why are you going so soon?" asked Mr. Smith-Tomkins gruffly.

"We never stay long anywhere. My uncle has a map, and he goes where that tells him. I've come to say goodbye early, because I thought we could have another long talk first."

Rollo settled himself down accordingly, and if Mr. Smith-Tomkins' tongue did not move very fast, he did duty for them both. Time slipped by, and suddenly the swish of the incoming tide made Rollo look round. To his consternation he found the waves had quietly crept in behind them, cutting them off entirely from the beach the other side of the projecting cliff.

"Oh, Mr. Smith-Tomkins, what shall we do? Where is Sims?"

"The fool is dawdling in the town, I suppose. He went to Rumelford to get something for me."

"Rumelford is a long way off, isn't it? We must get back at once, the tide is coming in all round us. I'll push your chair through the water, it can't be *very* deep yet."

Rollo was rising to the occasion, but his face was pale with apprehension. The chair was very heavy, and the beach stony. He managed to turn it round, but when the invalid saw the encroach that the sea had made, he uttered an exclamation of despair.

"Sims has left me here to die, run on yourself and leave me; I did tell that fool I wouldn't mind drowning. He wanted to move me before he went, but he'll be thankful to see the last of me. Leave me, boy, and go!"

Rollo shouted aloud for help, but the noise of the waves seemed to drown his voice. He struggled to push the chair through the water, but it stuck between the large stones and he could not dislodge it.

He turned and faced Mr. Smith-Tomkins solemnly.

"I believe God means us to die," he said. "And if He does I s'pose it will be all right."

"Leave me!" shouted Mr. Smith-Tomkins. "Try and wade through. Don't you see that is our only chance?"

Rollo saw at last, and splashed bravely through the water. Deeper and deeper it got; he turned his head and called out in an unnaturally cheerful tone, "I'll go on till it comes up to my mouth, and then I'll try to swim. I can nearly do that."

Mr. Smith-Tomkins watched him with eager blood-shot eyes. Why, oh, why did life seem so precious to him, when he led such a useless, miserable existence? He could not reason it out. His heart was full of a dull hopeless rage against his own impotence and helplessness. One little lad held his life in his hand, would he be able to get through and bring help in time?

Then Rollo gave a shout.

" I've got through the deepest bit. I'm all right now, I'll bring you help ! "

He disappeared round the corner. The invalid sat still and waited. The waves crept greedily around his chair, they lapped through the wheels of it, they dashed their foam into his face, and soon with a little splash and splutter filled the bottom of it. Higher and higher they rose. They began to buffet him to and fro, and the miserable man looked out upon the ocean with dread filling his soul. He was not ready to die, he kept repeating to himself ; he could not die so suddenly; he meant to be better before his time came. And then he looked up into the heavens above, and this prayer rose to his lips—

" I'll be different if I'm given another chance. May the Almighty give it to me, for Christ's sake. Amen."

Was that a voice, a cry ? He turned his head.

As his prayer ascended it was heard and answered. A boat was coming round the corner, and Rollo was waving and shouting to him.

A few minutes later he was being carefully lifted into the boat, and as he was taken to his house the faithful Sims came rushing down to the beach in agony of mind.

" I knewed I would be too late, I told the master so, but he were so terrible set on my leavin' him, and going into Rumelford. I told one o' you to have a look to the master; now why couldn't you 'a done it ? "

Mr. Smith-Tomkins was quite exhausted with his wetting and exposure. Rollo went in and changed his clothes, and then ran over to inquire how he was, but Sims would not let him see him, only said he was doing well. However, just after uncle and nephew had finished their evening meal, a message came over from Mr. Smith-Tomkins asking to see the boy.

Rollo went at once, and was shown into a bedroom where his friend lay in bed, looking more abject and miserable than ever. "Come here," he said; "and send Sims away."

"I'm so sorry you got so wet," said Rollo, "but I'm very glad we came in time, I was so afraid we should be too late. May I talk about it? You don't mind? Well, you see, they took so long to understand, and most of them had gone out fishing, and when we got the boat out I thought they would never get along! I don't mind telling you, but I knew that Jesus Christ was with us. I told you how He always comes with us everywhere. And I asked Him to make the boat go faster. I seemed to fancy"—here Rollo's blue eyes got misty and dreamy—"that He took an oar Himself. I half believe He did, for we got through the sea quicker!"

There was a silence, then the man took hold of the small hand, and said brokenly—

"I'm a rich man, and have no use for my money. You could weigh that well, for I would leave it to you. I have no kith or kin, and it would be worth your while. I want to keep you with me—tell your uncle so—not because you saved my life this afternoon, but I'm going to live on different lines, and you and I could do it better together."

Rollo stared at him, only partially understanding the drift of his words.

"I'm afraid I couldn't leave my uncle," he said slowly; "and, you see, my holiday will soon be coming to an end."

"Your schooling would be seen to; I'd give you a tutor. I'm a lonely man, and it would be a first-rate thing for you. I want some one to talk to me. I'm sick of Sims's 'Yes, sir,' and 'No, sir,'—sick to death of his voice. I'd bring you up like a son of my own— couldn't do more. Tell your uncle to come up and talk it over and settle it as soon as possible. Expect he'll be glad to have you off his hands. Didn't you tell me he wanted to get married?"

"Yes—but—but I'm afraid I don't quite understand. Do you want me to come and live with you altogether? Because I couldn't do that. I belong to father and mother, and they're coming back from India some day, and then I shall live with them."

Mr. Smith-Tomkins made an impatient movement with his head.

"Tell your uncle to come over and speak to me," he muttered. "At once too—the sooner the better."

So Lionel was summoned, and very surprised he was when Mr. Smith-Tomkins propounded his scheme. Very kindly but firmly, he refused to entertain such an idea for a minute, and though the invalid grew angry, impatient, and pathetic by turns, Lionel remained firm.

"He is my sister's only child, and a very delicate one. I thank you for your generous offer, but as his guardian in the place of his parents I tell you nothing would induce me to give my consent to such a plan."

And then Lionel walked off, and left Rollo to soothe and comfort the disconsolate old man.

"I'm very sorry, really. Would you like me to write you letters, and tell you all the places we go to? And

couldn't you, wouldn't you write to me sometimes? I
do love letters so, and I hardly ever get any."

"I wish I had never set eyes on you," said the invalid
in a surly manner. "You're like all others, only care
for those in health and strength."

"I like you very much, really I do. I always like ill
people. There was an old woman I used to go to see
in London with Miss Percy. She was doubled up with
rheumatism, but she was always smiling. She used to
say her body was a creaking rusty cage but her soul
would soon be out of it. You'll be glad when you get
to heaven, won't you? I've been wondering about
souls and bodies since I talked with a lady about it.
And I wonder if people die because their souls get so
big that they burst up their bodies! Miss Greening
said that your soul ought to go on growing after your
body stopped. I was thinking of a chicken in the egg,
you know, how the egg gets too small to hold it, and it
must burst through!"

Mr. Smith-Tomkins gazed at him in silence, then he
said with a little laugh—

"Well, we had a narrow squeak of going through that
experience to-day, but I can't say my soul is a big one,
in fact I doubt whether I have one at all."

"Oh, but you must have one, because God made us
with souls, didn't He? Do you think we should have
been sitting in heaven together this evening if the sea
had drowned us this afternoon?"

Mr. Smith-Tomkins made no reply. Rollo chatted
on, from things in heaven to things on earth, and
when his time came to go he declared that he "hadn't
half finished talking."

But he did what he very seldom did to any one. He shyly stooped over the old man and kissed him.

"Goodbye," he said; "and if you get to heaven before me, keep a place by your side for me, for I really should like to have some more talk with you so much."

He went, and Mr. Smith-Tomkins' eyes glistened strangely. "Never saw such a little chap. Wonder if by any chance I could get to believe in—in good things —must have a try, I suppose—as I promised—should have been a dead man if he hadn't been with me!"

"I've been thinking," said Rollo that evening to his uncle, just before he went to bed, "of another chapter our book must have. I think we might write about partings."

"What kind of partings?" asked Lionel lazily.

"All kinds—things and people coming to pieces. Your soul and your body parting, and saying goodbye to people, and—and chickens and eggs, and all the things you lose and never find again, like my pencil I had for two years, and I've never been able to buy another just like it since. I have got it rather confused in my head, but you could put it straight."

"Yes, we could have a chapter on parts and partings," assented his uncle. "Kingdoms, communities, families, and individuals all have parts that drop away from them, sometimes to their advantage, sometimes disadvantage. We must be willing to part with a good deal that is marring our whole, if we wish to obtain the 'better part.'"

"That's too difficult for me," sighed Rollo.

"And," pursued Lionel meditatively, "we must part to make a whole."

"Good-night," said Rollo meekly.

L

CHAPTER XVI

Their Book

"ROLLO, come here. I want to speak to you."

Rollo had finished his breakfast, and was gazing delightedly out of the window of a very substantial inn in an old-fashioned market town. It was market day, and the large square in front of the house was crowded with cattle, sheep, and country people in their carts, and on foot, with the inevitable market baskets on their arms.

Lionel and his little nephew had done a long tramp the day previously, so were having a late breakfast in consequence. It was ten o'clock, and Lionel was still sitting at the table with his cup of coffee untouched before him, wholly engrossed in his letters."

Rollo came at once when he was called.

"I am afraid our tramp must come to an end," Lionel said. "I have business that necessitates my return to town earlier than I thought, but I am feeling so fit now that I have no longer any excuse for staying away. What about you? Do you feel ready to go back to lessons again?"

"I'm quite well, thank you," said Rollo slowly; "I think I shall like it after a bit, you know."

Lionel looked at him critically.

"You are sunburnt and rosy," he said, "and have a good deal more flesh on your bones than when you started with me. I hope Miss Percy will be satisfied with you. We will have a look round this place for to-day, then to-morrow we will go by train to Exeter, give Dandy back to his master, and go on to town by the midday train."

"It is very quick news to me," said Rollo, staring at his uncle in a dazed fashion. "I somehow thought we would go on for ever, at least until all the summer went."

"Such was never my intention," said Lionel, smiling. "Now make the most of your last day. I thought we would take our lunch out, and visit the ruins of an old abbey on the top of a hill near here. But I have letters to write first. Run out of doors and amuse yourself for an hour, then I shall be ready."

Rollo put on his straw hat and went out. He felt a strange sinking at his heart, and the market-place for the time had lost its attraction.

He wandered through the town, then opened the gate of a field and went across it. When he came to the end of it, he found himself on the brow of a hill overlooking a wooded valley. The air blew across from the opposite hill sweet and fresh, birds were singing in those peculiar liquid mellow tones that show they are lazily enjoying their existence. Rollo leant across the bars of a gate and feasted his eyes and his soul upon the scene in front of him. The blue haze in the distance, the mingling of the larches, beeches, and elms in the woods, the soft contour of the hills, and the sparkle of the winding river below, all seemed to him to say—

" Stay with us ; we love you, and you love us."

Stretching out his small arms, he threw his head up, and drew in a long breath.

"Oh, you are beautiful, beautiful ! " he cried ; "why should I leave you? I hate smoky, foggy London, and I'm going back there to-morrow."   Then in the fulness of his heart he raised his eyes heavenwards.

" O God, this is your country.   I'm sure you can't like London ; do bring me back here ! You'll know how to manage it.   If only London could be swallowed up or buried like Sodom and Gomorrah without the people being burnt ! Please do help me to live in the country.   For Jesus Christ's sake.   Amen."

He was very silent when he returned to his uncle. Lionel seemed in good spirits. He informed his nephew that Miss Chesterfield and her uncle were returning to town the same day as they were.   " And I think we shall meet them at Exeter," he added, "so we may travel together."

"And then after the day after to-morrow," said Rollo lugubriously, " you and I will be quite away from each other, and won't know what the other is doing."

" I can pretty well guess at your occupation," Lionel said, with an amused look in his eye.   " I know your tongue will be pretty hard at it for the first day or two."

" But my soul," said Rollo slowly, " will be sorrowful."

Lionel looked at him.   The boy was walking steadily along, but his eyes were gazing into space, and his uncle checked the smile that came to his lips.

" You won't be sorry to see Miss Percy again, I am sure."

Rollo gave a little sigh.

"I have a country soul," he said; "I think God made me with one."

"But if you lived the life you have been leading with me all the year round you would run to weed, and when you grew up you would be unfit to take your place as a country gentleman anywhere. Learn all you can now, and trust that you may have the desire of your heart fulfilled when you grow to man's estate. Don't let this idle holiday make you discontented with your school duties, or I shall regret having taken you with me."

Rollo was silent.

They reached the old abbey, and here against an ivy-covered turret they sat down and ate their lunch. Rollo shook off his gravity and began to enjoy himself.

When Lionel lay down to have a smoke he took out a little well-worn notebook from his pocket, and began writing busily. Presently he said to his uncle—

"When shall we write our book?"

"Oh, ah! I had forgotten. What is it to be called?"

"I have the chapters written out. Shall I read them to you? The heads of chapters, I mean."

"Read away."

Rollo cleared his throat importantly.

"Chapter One: Golden Gorse."

"Chapter Two: Runaways."

"Chapter Three: Ends."

"Chapter Four: Worlds."

"Chapter Five: Bullies and Benefactors."

"Chapter Six: Messengers."

"Chapter Seven: Love."

"Chapter Eight: Growth."

"Chapter Nine : Parts and Partings."

"Very good," Lionel said thoughtfully. "We will take another holiday some time, my boy, and write that book together. I think we might add one more chapter."

"What shall it be?"

"I must think it out and tell you later on. Do you think you have learnt much from our tramp?"

"I have found out that the world is very big," said Rollo. "You see, I have seen and spoken to such quantities of people, and I like them all, every one of them. No one has been disagreeable to me or called me a boy."

"But is that an objectionable truth?"

"It means in London that you're a plague. Miss Percy says that boys have got a name for being troublesome. I've made a list in my book of the people I would like to see again. Would you like to hear it?"

"Yes."

So Rollo read—

"Fay.

"Mrs. Duncan.

"Bobby.

"Kizzy.

"Alf.

"Miss Greening.

"Mr. Smith-Tomkins.

"Those are my friends," he added in conclusion; "and now I'll tell you what I should like. I should like father and mother to come home and have a very big house in the country. Kizzy would be our housekeeper and Alf our coachman. Miss Greening would have one

big spare room, and Mrs. Duncan another, and Mr.
Smith-Tomkins another. Fay and Bobby would do
lessons with me, and play. And then you would have
the study and be writing our book; and—and "—Rollo
looked shyly at his uncle—" I think Miss Chesterfield
would have to stay with us too."

" A very happy family," laughed Lionel; "but I
should be sorry for the head of such a household."

They chatted on; then got up and explored the old
abbey, and tried to piece its past walls and passages
together. When they returned to the inn, packing was
done, and then in the cool of the evening they sauntered
down to an old stone bridge across the river. Here they
sat and had more desultory conversation.

" One wonders," said Lionel musingly, " if the footprints we leave behind us as we tramp through life guide
or mislead. It would be good to be one's own follower
sometimes."

" Do we always leave footprints behind us?" asked
Rollo with interest.

" Always."

" Have we in Devonshire?"

" Yes."

This sent Rollo into a brown study. He emerged
from it with a shining face.

" Is Jesus Christ in front of us or behind as we go
along? "

" In front, I hope; if we keep in our right position
He is."

" Then if we keep close behind Him, our footprints
will guide other people after Him, won't they?"

Lionel smiled assent.

"Our last chapter in our book must be on Footprints, I think."

"And what shall we call our book itself?"

Lionel thought.

"Tramps and their Guide," he said.

Rollo clasped his hands over his knees and looked up into the sky. The sun was slowly setting, and sending shafts of crimson and gold along the horizon as it did so. There was a stillness in the air ; night was taking day softly and tenderly into his embrace, and Nature hushed her children to sleep in the process.

"I can't be a tramp in the country any more," he said slowly and reflectively; "but I shall never give up tramping after Jesus."